Praise for

The Church of Wrestling

"*The Church of Wrestling* is a short, powerful novella about the ways losses can be shared and the ways they cannot. A story told through layers of nostalgia that are never sentimental, Emily Thomas Mani's deft prose paints an authentic portrait of found family helping each other through their trauma and grief, clinging to the past in the face of an uncertain future. A wonderful debut."

—Michael Melgaard, author of *Pallbearing*

"We are all grappling with something, but rarely has an author more aptly captured wrestling as a metaphor or as a filter through which to understand grief, family, and faith than Emily Thomas Mani in *The Church of Wrestling*. The narrator learns early that it's worth a lot of points to throw an opponent, and so too does Thomas Mani expertly send readers flying through unexpected circumstances that persistently subvert expectations. There's the rush of a surprising outcome to an early wrestling match, the twist of abject loss making the protagonist a better student, the peace that comes from bootleg VHS recordings of popular TV shows, and—perhaps least likely of all—the ways in which a half-baked new religion might succeed at drawing people together. Thomas Mani's is a story worth reading and rereading to study its craft and see if you can trace every first strike, counter, and reversal en route to the final pin."

—Michael Chin, author of *My Grandfather's an Immigrant and So is Yours* and *Circus Folk*

"What a gem of a book. Thomas Mani gets the experience of being a child exactly right, as few writers can, in all its comforts, traumas, and absurdities, without condescension or sentimentality. *The Church of Wrestling* grows into a moving depiction of loss while retaining its subtle, sideways sense of humor, through a story that's unexpected at every turn."

—Kim Fu, author of *The Lost Girls of Camp Forevermore*

"Thomas Mani inhabits the remarkable world of a girl navigating grief, life and love, while achingly bearing witness to those who wrestle with the uncontrollable. This acutely observed and deftly handled debut not only illuminates an extraordinary life, but also shines a light on a literary talent to watch."

—Sarah Meehan Sirk, author of *The Dead Husband Project*

"In *The Church of Wrestling*, Emily Thomas Mani deconstructs the concept of family. Through a child's eyes—forced to see through an adult lens—it becomes clear that those who take care of us and those who care for us most aren't always the same people at the same time."

—Mila Jaroniec, author of *Plastic Vodka Bottle Sleepover*

The Church of Wrestling

a novella

Emily Thomas Mani

Published by Split/Lip Press
6710 S. 87th St.
Ralston, NE 68127
www.splitlippress.com

ISBN: 978-1-952897-15-3

Cover Design by David Wojciechowski

Author Photo by Alyssa Bistonath

Editing by Kate Finegan

For my dad

The day before the tournament in Toronto, we found my mother in the hospital. We were both wearing our sweatsuits because it was my dad's opinion that an athlete should stay loose in the days leading up to a big event. He said that if your body feels loose then your mind will feel loose.

I wasn't nervous about seeing her until we got to her room, then I hesitated in the door frame. Her eyes were closed. She was hooked up to a breathing machine.

My dad walked up to the foot of the bed and put his hands on the rail, looking her over. He was a little breathless because we had rushed in from the parking lot and all down the hallway.

"It's her," he said.

I took a couple of steps into the room for a better look. Her face was partly obscured by the breathing tube. A hospital blanket was tucked around her body, so tightly that I could make out her shape.

"She's almost my size," I said. "The same weight class."

I took a couple more steps until I was right next to her and put my hand on her chest.

"I don't think you're supposed to do that," said my dad.

"But I want to see if it feels the same."

My dad cleared his throat. "I think we should talk to her."

I took my hand away. "But she's unconscious."

"She can still hear us, though. I read that somewhere."

"I don't want to talk."

"That's okay. I'll talk." My dad nodded to assure me that it really was okay. He cleared his throat again and straightened up like he was about to give a speech. Then he said her name.

I turned away. He'd only said that name a couple of times in my whole life and I always turned away. It was a reflex.

"It's me," he said. "It's Billy. And Jenny's here too."

I felt embarrassed and put my hands into my pockets. I didn't want to be acknowledged.

"She's a wrestler now," he said.

"Dad?"

He looked at me, waiting. I wanted to tell him that this was weird and that he should stop, that I didn't like it. I just wanted to leave the hospital and get ready for my tournament. But I couldn't say any of it, couldn't make my mouth work. So he turned back to my mother.

"She has a tournament tomorrow and I'm sure she's going to win. She even has two other girls to wrestle."

So, there would be three of us. A whole gold, silver, and bronze medals' worth of girls. When I wrestled boys, I would be on the podium on top of a dozen wrestlers. With girls, it was often just two of us.

"They're good," he said. "But not as good as her."

"Really?" I said. "Can I use another principle then?"

He looked at my mother like he didn't want to argue in front of her. That's how I knew what he was going to say before he said it.

"I already told you to stick to the first one, Kidlet. And I mean it. No use trying another principle on these kids. One day you'll meet your match."

"But I'm bored of Strike First."

"I know. But you need a worthy opponent to grow."

"But I don't have a worthy opponent," I said. "And what if I never do?"

We watched the violent rise and fall of my mother's chest. It wasn't smooth like breathing should be. It was a quick sucking in and letting out, like a punch.

"What if I never get to learn a new principle ever, in my whole life?"

"Then you'll have mastered Strike First better than anyone."

It was simple and straightforward to him, but I could feel frustration swelling beyond its usual size to the point that I couldn't ignore it.

"What about Counter Attack?" I asked. "Please? I want to get better so badly."

My dad smiled his gentle smile. He didn't say anything but I could read his mind. *That's why you're such a good wrestler, Kidlet.*

A doctor peeked her head into the room, keeping her body mostly in the hallway. "Are you the family?"

"Family?" said my dad. The word startled him. "I guess so."

The doctor referred to her clipboard. "Are you Mr. Arsenault?"

"Right, yes, that's me. I'm sorry. We are the family, but it's been a while."

"You're the emergency contact though, right?"

I had to look away from his face while he thought about this. "I guess she never got around to changing it," he said.

The doctor glanced at me, her mouth crooked. I wasn't used to being looked at that way. "Mr. Arsenault, can I see you in the hall?"

"Yep," he said, and looked at me. "Keep talking to her, okay?"

He disappeared into the hallway with the doctor, closing the door until there was just a crack and I couldn't hear what they were saying.

I had a vague understanding that this moment was very important and I should feel something. But I felt very little, aside from the discomfort of being in the room alone with her. Watching the machine help her breathe made me too aware of my own breathing so that I had to concentrate on inhaling and exhaling and pausing in between. I started to feel lightheaded.

A nurse came into the room and, without acknowledging me, rounded the bed to check the machines and IV bag. She looked at her watch, then pulled a pen lid off with her teeth and signed the chart at the bottom of the bed, noting the time beside it. She put the lid back on.

"Are you okay in here by yourself?" she said, finally looking at me.

"Yes," I said, because I was always okay.

"Isn't this your mother?" she asked.

"Yes, but we're not close. I haven't seen her in eleven years."

She looked at me like the doctor had. "How old are you?"

"I'm eleven," I said, and right away I heard how bad that sounded. It all sounded bad.

"Do you want to watch TV?" She pointed to the bedside table and the remote. There was a television mounted to the corner of the ceiling. "Sometimes the family thinks it's disrespectful. But why should you sit here in silence?"

"They told us she might die," I said. "We're supposed to prepare for the worst."

The nurse handed me the remote. "Sometimes it's nice to have the company."

I felt an immediate liking for this nurse, who spoke with such conviction like her words were all planned out.

"I have a lot of experience with this situation," she said.

I nodded and she seemed to take this as permission to go, like she'd left the room in better shape than she found it.

I turned on the television. It was already on channel eleven, *The Price is Right* and the Showcase Showdown. I sat down in a chair beside the bed and looked at my mother's closed eyes, checking for a little twitch, or a flutter of the lids, or any change at all.

I watched as Bob Barker and the models told the last two contestants—Leonard and Linda—what they had in store.

"Most contestants hope for a car," I said under my breath, too quiet for my mother to hear. "But I would hope for a trip."

The first item on the Showcase Showdown was a pinball machine. I guess old pinball machines are worth a lot of money because Leonard seemed really excited about it and I doubted he actually played pinball. Not too many people do. It's boring. The second item was a brand-new home gym. There were models working out on all the equipment.

"Yeah right," I said. "They don't have any muscle mass. I doubt they ever go to the gym. They probably lie around all day drinking champagne."

I had heard somewhere that models did that. It's how they stayed so skinny.

The third item on the Showcase Showdown was a camper. Not quite a car and not quite a trip, I thought, sort of in between. Leonard went berserk jumping around. Then all of a sudden, he stopped and looked very stressed out, deliberating the price.

I turned to my mother. I looked at the wires coming out of

her hospital gown. Through the thin fabric, I could make out the electrodes. They were taped to her chest but they looked as though they went inside of her. I put my hand on top of everything and even through all the layers, I could feel it.

"I have a plan," I said.

I wanted to tell her what the plan was, but I started to feel lightheaded again. The reflex happened and I turned away and looked at the TV. So I told Bob Barker, instead. I told Leonard.

"I'm going to use another principle tomorrow," I said.

Leonard jumped in triumph. He'd won the Showcase Showdown. He'd only been off by twenty-nine bucks.

My dad came back into the room. He wasn't out of breath anymore but he looked exhausted. He seemed to have trouble meeting my eyes. He looked at my hand instead, still on my mother's chest. I didn't say anything but he could read my mind. *It feels the same. I knew it was real.*

When I was born, he was still young, just twenty years old with a robust mustache. In his wrestling singlet, he was ripped and small like Freddie Mercury. It was the summer of 1980, and my dad, Billy Arsenault, was at the height of a miraculous, undefeated wrestling career. He'd won the Canadian Championship twice and a gold at the PanAm games the year before. He and his friends and his coaches and everyone my dad knew were still holding out hope for the Moscow Olympics. Maybe something in the political air would shift. Maybe Canada would lift their boycott. My dad trained, hard and hoping, right up until July 19.

"And then you came along," he said. "Concurrent with the opening ceremony." He would pause, as though referring to notes, written and kept in the sky. "That's when I knew!" he said abruptly like *aha!* Like a twist in the story because to him, it was. My birth coinciding with the opening ceremony was the first hint of the meaningfulness of his sport, the way it intertwined with reality.

Wrestling was ordained. It was a narrative.

As soon as I was born, my mother got depressed.

"No," my dad would clarify. "It was a few days after you were born. When the milk came in." He would look at me to make sure I understood. "She got . . . lost. Inside the mind." He touched a finger to his temple. That's where the mind was.

"I understand," I would say. "And then what happened?"

"Then I took her to the hospital."

"And then what?"

He would raise his eyebrows and smile his gentle smile that I loved because it made me feel like things weren't all bad. What happened to my mother was bad, but there was always me. And I was good.

"Then it was just us," he would say. It was a sort of conclusion. My mother never really came back.

I picture my dad then, alone with a newborn and trying to figure out the baby formula, watching the tail end of the Olympics. Maybe he wished he was in Moscow instead of at home with me. Maybe he imagined the other reality, the one where my mother was at home with the newborn, and he was in Moscow wrestling Ilya Anoshkin in the gold medal match. Maybe he grieved that version.

As it was, Ilya won gold in the 68kg category, my dad's weight class. Uncle Mike, who wasn't really my uncle but my dad's coach, acquired a videotape of Ilya and the two of them watched it obsessively, concluding in new ways how my dad would have won gold if Canada had competed. After one of the matches, there's an interview with Ilya and a Soviet reporter. They speak in Russian until the very end, when Ilya looks straight into the camera and says in English, gleefully, "Soviet Union is number one! Wrestling is number one!"

"Why is he speaking in English?" I asked.

"Because he's sending the West a message," said Uncle Mike.

"What's the message?"

"The message is about communism."

"Huh?"

"No," said my dad. "The message is about wrestling."

"But what *about* wrestling?"

"That it's everything," he said, transfixed by his opponent, looking into Ilya's eyes like he was in the room, transcending the television screen. And truly, Ilya seemed to look back at him, somehow connecting through time and space.

Ilya was the worthy opponent my dad never had the chance to beat. He was the one that got away. Because after my birth and the Moscow Olympics, my dad quit wrestling to take care of me. He found a house, just down the street from Uncle Mike, in the Toronto suburb of Brampton. It was in a small subdivision, just built. The houses were close together and dozens of kids were always outside playing. They ignored the traffic, so my dad would have to honk his horn to clear a way. Uncle Mike opened his own wrestling club in the northeast end of the city, where you could see the CN Tower on a clear day, and took my dad on as head coach. We spent all our time there, Uncle Mike and various mothers carrying me around in their arms and feeding me my bottles while my dad coached the boys. There was a strict rule about the age of the wrestlers.

"Six years old at the very youngest," said my dad. "But you were only four. Uncle Mike broke the rule for you."

"Because I beat Joshua Cooper," I said. We used to say that Joshua was my first opponent but it was kind of a joke. He was another wrestler at the gym who was like my big brother. He was playing around with me once and I tackled him because that was what everyone else was doing.

"Also," I said, "Uncle Mike let me wrestle just because he loves me so much."

Uncle Mike was a steady presence in our lives. Sometimes I saw the boys look at him, and I could tell that they were a little afraid. He was direct and intimidating, but not with me. While my dad was emotional and prone to phases, Uncle Mike was consistent both day-to-day and year-to-year. I'd only known him in a crisp, collared polo tee, whether he was going to the gym or a funeral. It accompanied the plain, sensible aesthetic of his entire wardrobe, his steadfast fitness and clean house, his crew-cut hair.

Also, I'd only known him to be single. I could only recall him going on one date in my entire life. If there were more, my dad and I were never introduced, but I always had the sense that to Uncle Mike, romantic love was not worth the mess.

He taped all my matches with a camcorder so we could study them. Watching them later at home, I would hear the comments he made to himself behind the camera. *Get 'em, Jenny! Way to go, honey!*

Whenever I beat a boy, Uncle Mike would make his hand into a fist and throw it in the air. *Get a load of her!*

The mothers of the boys I was wrestling weren't as enthusiastic. While they admitted I was good, I was an anomaly. I was a different kind of girl, abandoned by her mother and raised by men, raised inside the gym. I had short hair because my dad didn't know how to work a hair elastic. I would, the women said, quit wrestling when I turned thirteen or fourteen, or whenever all that stuff happened. I would quit wrestling and become a girl, a real one. They couldn't see that my girlhood was already real and happening alongside the wrestling, even when I made my dad take me to the mall to get my ears pierced with tiny synthetic ruby earrings because that was my birthstone, even when I painted my nails with sparkly purple nail polish and wore pink sweatpants over my wrestling singlet. They saw the "girly" things as proof of something on the inside trying to get out, even though they were already on the outside.

Boys were easy opponents because they didn't expect a girl to be very good, so I would take them by surprise and win quickly. All I had to do was strike first. This was the only principle my dad ever let me use. Strike First, on the mat and off. I was supposed to tackle my opponent the second the whistle blew, the *millisecond* the whistle blew. Most boys were so disoriented by that first hard tackle that they never recovered. They were used to circling around their opponent for half a minute before engaging. Even the ones who managed to fight back didn't have enough breath left in them to win. Strike First was my dad's answer to everything. If messiness was encroaching on my room, my dad would refuse my offer to clean up tomorrow.

"Strike First, Kidlet, don't let the mess catch its breath."

If I had a bad spelling quiz at school, he made me see my teacher for extra help right away, which was embarrassing. For most kids, one bad quiz went almost unnoticed. Even my teacher thought I was a keener.

"He doesn't want to be blindsided again," said Uncle Mike. "He wants to be the one in control."

"What do you mean *again*?" I asked. "When was the first time?"

"You and your questions," he said. "You just like asking them, even when you know the answer."

I looked at him indignantly but I knew that he was right. Deep down inside of me where the reflex was, I knew that he was talking about my mother. "Well, what does *blindsided* even mean then? Can you at least tell me *that*?"

"As if you don't know. It's when you don't even see it coming."

"See what coming?"

"The punch." He pretended to punch himself, slow motion, in the side of the face.

"Or the tackle," I said.

"The danger, Jenny. Any kind of danger. If you strike first, you're in control. That's what your dad always taught you. It's why you're so good."

But my dad wouldn't let me use the other principles, except in practice. He was worried it would mar my technique. How could I properly learn Endurance if all my matches were over in two minutes? How could I learn Counter Attack if the initial attacks were subpar?

None of the other principles mattered, because Strike First led to a quick and certain win. To my boy opponents, this was unforgivable. Sometimes they would refuse to shake my hand after I won and my dad would rage and make Uncle Mike talk to their coach, who would agree to add a point to my total on account of the grievance.

"Being a gracious loser is just as important as being a gracious winner," my dad told me after one of these incidents. "Remember that, Kidlet."

"How would you know?" I said. "You've never lost before."

Then Uncle Mike piped up and said that I was like my dad, I always won my matches. "But it's still a good lesson to keep in mind, honey. Especially when you're wrestling girls."

Uncle Mike understood that in some ways, girls were more difficult to beat because they approached each match with caution, not cockiness. When I beat them and we shook hands I always wanted to say, *but don't worry, it's okay, we're both good*. Then the tournament would end and I would mourn the going home, even with my gold medal. I pictured the other girls going home as well and wondered if they had friends like them, girls who wrestled, girls with mothers who cheered from the stands.

My dad and I had stopped talking about my mother.

There was a photograph of her, taken when she was pregnant with me. My dad kept it on a high shelf, in his office at the gym. It had been there since the beginning, I thought. Now it was dusty, unmoved.

"Dad?" I asked. "When did she hold me?"

He looked at me, jarred. "When you were born, she held you. They put you in her arms. The doctors did. Why?"

"Nothing."

"Tell me," he said. "You can tell me."

I didn't like what was happening to his face. It was like he was looking inside of me, but not in a good way.

"I just remember it," I said, quietly.

"That's impossible, you were too little," he shook his head and relaxed a bit, relieved to go off topic. "Scientists don't really understand why we can't remember events from when we were babies. You didn't have language so you couldn't store memories properly. That's one theory."

"But I remember the sound of her heart. So it's real."

"No, it's not real. This is real," he said, pointing to the photo. "This is real. She's happy. She how happy she is?"

I turned away from his face. Since I couldn't see it, I didn't cry. "I understand," I said.

I never asked about her again. I never asked about the blindsiding because I only wanted my dad to smile. When he smiled, I had everything I wanted. Our life was good. It was the same all the time. Every Friday we went down the street to Uncle Mike's house to order pizza for dinner. They let me watch *TGIF* while they talked in the kitchen, Uncle Mike drinking Coors Light and my dad drinking can after can of Coca-Cola. I would fall asleep on the couch and wake up hours later in the very early morning, at 1:00 AM, maybe 2:00. Uncle Mike and my dad would be close to the television, volume turned down low, watching old wrestling matches of my dad's, everything leading up to 1980. Then they would watch Ilya in hushed voices, bodies moving with the wrestlers onscreen and at a certain point, Uncle Mike would turn to my dad and whisper.

"That's where you would have had him."

I was happy because I was little. I had pizza. I had my dad and Uncle Mike and I had wrestling. I was undefeated.

On the morning of the tournament in Toronto, my dad drove me downtown. We would meet up with Uncle Mike and our team at the arena.

"You're not thinking about it, are you?" my dad asked.

"Thinking about what?"

For a moment, I thought he knew about my plan. Then I realized he was talking about my mother and the hospital.

He looked at me quietly for a second like he was going to say it out loud. "Nothing," he said. "I just want you to be focused."

"I'm always focused."

We went into the arena and found Uncle Mike and the rest of our team. While my dad pointed out my opponents, I ate a Snickers bar and tried not to look him in the face. Three girls in my weight class meant three matches. We would each wrestle one another and then the top two would wrestle again for the gold. There was nothing particularly notable about the other girls. Of course, they were my size and a little bit nervous. I saw them eyeing me like I was eyeing them, although it's likely they knew something about me, had heard that I was impossible to beat. I decided that for my first two matches, I would use Strike First as usual. In the gold medal match, I would stage my rebellion: Counter Attack. I would let the other girl put a move on me, then I would counter.

After the weight check, everyone dispersed to different corners of the arena to wait for their matches to start. My first match was about a half-hour away so I settled into the stands to watch my teammates and cheer them on. With each match, I got more and more into it and eventually moved from the stands to the corner of the mat, yelling encouragement and instructions.

"Rip it off!" I screamed, when my teammate's opponent had him in a half nelson. "Rip his hand off!" I sounded furious and frightening. I caught my future opponent watching me and grinned.

Uncle Mike came over and told me to quiet down a bit.

"Your teammates can hear *you* but they can't hear the actual instructions. "He pointed to my dad. "They can't hear the coach."

I shrugged and started pulling off my gold quilted sweatsuit because I was up next. Uncle Mike squeezed my shoulders then pounded my back with a *thump, thump, thump.*

"Go get 'em, honey," he said. "Put all that energy to good use. Put it where it's going to hurt." He made some kind of battle gesture with his fist, his other hand clutching his camcorder.

I walked out onto the mat. I shook my opponent's hand, then I smiled at my dad before the whistle blew and *bam*, the girl and I were on the ground and I had pinned her.

My second match went just as well. Afterward, I put my sweatsuit on and asked my dad for five dollars for the concession stand.

"What are you going to buy?" he asked.

"Pepperoni pizza."

My dad pulled out his wallet and then stopped, a five-dollar bill half-out. He looked up at me.

"Maybe you should wait until after your match," he said.

"Why?" I asked, and I could hear the demand in my voice, the entitlement.

"Because you don't seem like yourself today. You seem off your game."

"But I pinned both girls right away," I said, tilting my head. It was an uncharacteristic cockiness and I knew I was being a brat.

"I think you should wait," my dad said. "You need to focus. This is important."

I sighed, crossing my gold-quilted arms and going to sit in the bleachers to wait out my last match. I didn't cheer on my teammates. I didn't stretch. I just sat in my indignation. By the time my number was up, I was good and ready to defy my dad.

I stripped off my sweatsuit for the third time and walked out onto the mat without looking at him. By then he might have suspected I was up to something but was trying to pretend that everything was going as planned. He kept clapping his hands together like *all right, let's do this.*

"Strike first, Jenny!" he yelled. "Just strike first!"

It wasn't until I shook my opponent's hand that I felt any trepidation at all. In that second before the whistle blew, I wondered if I was going to make a mistake. But the referee brought his hand down and the match started and it felt too late to deliberate. I did as planned. I circled my opponent, something I'd never done before. I heard my dad still yelling, "Strike, Jenny! Strike!" But we just kept circling.

"Engage, wrestlers," the referee ordered. Then my opponent came at me, wrapping an arm around my head and grabbing my shoulder with both hands. She threw me down.

It was amazing. I knew just what to do. We'd practiced it more times than I could count. I let my opponent throw me onto my back so that she was on top of me, then I kept the momentum going until I was on top of her.

"Ohh!" the crowd cried, all in unison, completely surprised. It was not a counter-attack that they were used to seeing. I was now in a position to pin her, but she was resisting and I wasn't trying very hard. I was thinking about how good it felt to wrestle, to really wrestle and use the moves I'd practiced.

The referee finally blew the whistle and brought us back to the center to reset. I could hear my teammates yelling out instructions but wasn't listening to what they were saying. My dad must have been yelling too. He must have been. But I didn't hear it.

We began again, and my opponent came at me for a throw just like before. I used the exact same counter-attack and was on top of her for a second time.

"Ohh!" came the cry again.

I thought that my opponent must use that throw the same way I used Strike First. It was her go-to principle. It was her sure thing, and here I was countering it, twice in a row. She must feel destabilized, I thought. She must be doubting her training and her coaching. I felt more powerful than I'd ever felt with Strike First.

The referee blew the whistle again and brought us back to the center. I was sure I was going to win. Everyone was shouting my name. I heard my dad.

"Jenny," he yelled, which was exactly what everyone else was shouting but it made me turn to him. "Jenny!" He was pointing to the scoreboard. It was 6–4 for my opponent. "Jenny, you have to strike first! You have to pin her!"

But I seemed to have forgotten everything. I forgot how to strike first. I forgot how to pin. My opponent was looking at my dad, then she looked at me and the whistle blew. A millisecond later, she tackled me with a double leg takedown. I knew I was in danger of being pinned. I felt destabilized. I doubted everything, but I kept my shoulders up. She was looking down at me and I knew that she had stolen my principle.

I ran down the clock with my shoulders up. The referee blew the whistle to end the match and the other girl got up. She went to the center of the mat to be declared winner, but I couldn't move. I'd collapsed on my back, exhausted. I wasn't used to matches ending without the euphoria of victory. My dad was over in my corner and I turned to him. He wasn't even trying to smile. It was the worst thing I'd ever seen. Everything else in the arena disappeared. It was just me and my dad, disappointed.

"Wrestlers," said the ref. "Shake hands."

I turned away from my dad and managed to get up. It was a strange walk to the center of the mat because my body was numb.

I barely registered the rest of the tournament. Somehow, I ended up on the podium on the second-place tier, accepting a silver medal. I looked down at it, inspecting it like a curiosity, then let it fall to my chest.

Afterward, my teammates traipsed off to the bus and Uncle Mike, following them, clapped me on my back with the same *thump, thump, thump*. It was nearly identical to what he always did, but watching him board the bus I wondered if he still loved me.

It was dark and for a while, in the car with my dad, the city lights were a distraction. Somewhere in my mind, I knew that I had changed and something difficult was about to spill out of me and I wouldn't be able to put it back in. But there seemed to be a few minutes where I could defer all that and just watch the city and the people that lived there. My dad had bought me a slice of pepperoni pizza, but it sat on my lap getting cold on the paper plate.

My dad finally spoke. "You know what happened, right?"

"No."

"A throw is worth more points than the counter."

"Oh," I said, and I heard all the emotion in my voice and it made me feel small. The tears were coming and I tried to stop them because I knew they wouldn't just come a little bit.

"It's okay," he said. "We'll study Uncle Mike's tape later. You'll see where you went wrong."

"I don't want to."

"You have to," said my dad. "You have to learn from this. You have to learn that you can't win a match with counter-attacks. You win a match with attacks."

I closed my eyes.

"I would have known that if you had taught me," I said, and I knew these were the words before the tears. Crying would come when the words stopped, so I kept talking. "If you had let me try a different principle, if you had told me what principle to try then I would have known and I wouldn't have made a mistake and I wouldn't have lost and I would still be . . ." My eyes were closed. The tears were going to come and I wanted one more second, two seconds. "I would still be . . ."

I didn't get the last word out before it turned into something loud, turned into a wail. I could feel the tears on my face.

"You would still be undefeated," my dad said, over my crying, "if you had listened to me. I'm your coach and I told you to strike first. You always strike first."

"No," I yelled, tightening my hands into fists and shaking them. I stomped my feet in the little space in front of the passenger seat. "Strike first doesn't work. It doesn't work in life. How do you . . ." I turned to him and his face showed that he knew what I was thinking. But I said it anyway. I screamed it like he was to blame, even though I was to blame, unmistakably and unretractably. "How do you strike first at dying?"

My dad drove and I cried. The entire way home I cried. And the entire way home he didn't answer me but I knew what he was thinking. *I don't know. I don't know. I don't know.* I cried while we pulled into the driveway and walked into the house, cold pizza clutched in my hand, winter coat falling off my shoulders. I cried sitting on the couch while my dad checked the answering machine. I cried while he called the hospital back, taking the phone around the corner, the cord stretched taut. He was trying to whisper but really, it's difficult to whisper on the phone, especially when the other end is a busy hospital.

"I understand. I understand. Was she in a lot of pain?"

I failed him. That's how I saw it. For the next few days, as my dad called around making funeral arrangements, I avoided him. I didn't want to talk to him and figured he didn't want to talk to me. I stayed in my room, burying my silver medal at the bottom of my drawer and later that night, fishing it out again to flush down the toilet. It didn't fit, of course. It got stuck in the bowl while the ribbon fluttered, trying to drag it down with each flush. It didn't go down the toilet but it was sullied, which was good too.

By the time of the funeral, I hadn't really had human contact in three days. Uncle Mike wrapped me in a hug and I asked, "Do you still love me?"

"Of course," he said, but then drew back, confused. "What do you mean?"

I buried my face back into his chest. I thought about the silver medal, under the sink in the bathroom.

After the funeral, Uncle Mike came with us back to the house. I curled up with him on the couch and my dad slumped in the La-Z-Boy, looking like he would never move again.

"You should take a break," said Uncle Mike. "Maybe a couple of weeks. Jenny too."

I sat up straight and turned to look at him. "A break from what?"

"The gym."

I hadn't considered that wrestling would continue to be a part of our lives. I'd felt an undeniable end. I was completely and certainly finished, and at that moment felt an utter panic that my dad was not.

"But I quit wrestling," I said. "For good."

"You did what?"

"And Dad, you have to quit too because I can't . . ."

I didn't know how to finish the sentence. When I thought about wrestling, I wanted to disappear. I saw my dad's face at the tournament when I was losing and he was pointing at the scoreboard and he was disappointed and sad.

"But it's how I make money," he said.

"I want you to come with me." I expected him to know what I meant. He tilted his head to the side, trying.

"You're a good wrestler," said Uncle Mike. "It was just one match. You're good."

Their voices were far away. My thoughts went to the future and how to survive if wrestling was a part of it.

"I'm not good," I said. "I lost."

I picked up the remote and turned on the television, volume up high. It was late, and all I could find was *Law & Order*.

"We didn't even watch the tape," my dad said.

"Dad, if we watch the tape I'll die."

It was the most extreme threat I could think of, and I sort of believed it. If I ever wrestled again, I would die of sadness.

Two weeks later, my dad returned to the gym and I didn't. The only reason he let me stay home was because he was so sure I would change my mind. He thought I would realize my mistake. He thought I would miss it too much. But instead of talking about that, we talked about the rules. I wasn't allowed to answer the door. I wasn't allowed to answer the phone, except at 6:00 PM when he called to check on me. I did my homework and kept the television on the entire time. For dinner, he would leave a peanut butter sandwich on the counter with a bag of Ruffles. In the fridge there would be a glass of milk. He poured it for me, even though I could do it myself.

At 8:30 PM my dad would come home and sit on the La-Z-Boy and try to talk to me about the gym.

"I can't listen to this, Dad," I would say, shutting my eyes. "Talk about something else."

But there was nothing else. Our whole relationship had been about wrestling. So I just turned the TV up instead.

In the mornings, I would find him in the La-Z-Boy, half awake and halfway through a can of Coke. I don't think he slept. When he saw me he would jump up, plug in the toaster for my breakfast and start packing my lunch, usually more sandwiches and baggies full of grapes and Froot Loops. He was always trying so hard to seem okay, but even his *have a good day at school* was strained. He would pat me on the back hesitantly, like we didn't know each other anymore.

It was different with Uncle Mike. He understood that I didn't want to talk about wrestling. He asked about school or television. There were no more late-night viewings of the Ilya video, or any other wrestling videos, so we watched police procedurals instead. Sometimes there was a marathon.

"I don't know how you watch this stuff," said my dad. "It's so dark."

"I don't mind that it's dark," I said.

"I get it," said Uncle Mike. "It's a good distraction."

"No, it's not. It's interesting. I don't need a distraction."

My dad got up from the La-Z-Boy with his empty Coke can. "Mike, want another?" He went into the kitchen without waiting for a response. I was trying to focus on the TV, where they were about to catch the perp, but I could feel Uncle Mike looking at me. I lay down with my head against the arm of the couch and pulled a blanket up to my chin, trying to block him out.

"You know it's not your fault, right?" he said, trying to keep his voice down.

"Huh?"

"Your dad. He's sad because your mom died. Not because of you."

I pulled the blanket up more until it made a little tent around my eyes. All I could see was the television. "Can you turn the volume up?" I said. "Something's about to happen."

My dad returned with Uncle Mike's Coors Light and another can of Coke. He settled into his chair.

"Billy," said Uncle Mike. "I heard about a grief group that happens over at the United church."

I heard a hiss as my dad opened his Coke. There was a beat of quiet as he took a long first sip.

"It's on Tuesday evenings," said Uncle Mike. "You want to give it a try?"

"I'm at the gym on Tuesday evenings."

"I could manage without you for a couple hours."

I sat up. "Can everyone please be quiet?"

"We're talking," said Uncle Mike, annoyed. "That's the point of being together."

I found the remote and turned up the volume a few notches. Uncle Mike turned back to my dad.

"It's for people who have lost a spouse before the age of forty," he said.

"Huh?" I said. "What does age have to do with it?"

"I guess if you lose a spouse early, there are different things you want to talk about," my dad said.

My poor dad, I thought. He didn't even know why he was sad. But I liked the idea that we could pinpoint his grief, the size of it, on something as simple as his age. It had nothing to do with me, or my failure at the tournament. It had nothing to do with wrestling.

"I don't think I'll go," said my dad. "Especially if it means I get home even later than I do now."

"I think you should," I said. "Maybe it would be good for you to do . . . something else."

"Really?"

He hadn't looked at me like that in a while. I saw something hopeful flicker across his face and I felt a wave of guilt that I'd caused him so much grief. It had been months since I had really looked at him and I noticed he had a brand-new wrinkle, coming out the side of his eye like a lightning bolt.

"Go to the group, Dad. I want you to."

The morning after my dad's first grief group session, I came downstairs to find him standing at the stove, cooking.

"Dad? What are you doing?"

"I'm making a marinade," he said. "Lemon chicken."

"Lemon chicken," I said like it was a different language. My dad had never really cooked before.

"Grief group," said my dad, stirring the pot with a wooden spoon. "One of the women there was talking about food, and how you can sort of get into a rut with it. You can keep yourself in a certain stage of grief by just eating to get by instead of trying to enjoy your food." He tapped the wooden spoon on the edge of the pot then placed it down on the stove and threw open the oven door, retrieving a warmed plate.

"Breakfast," he said.

It was toast and scrambled eggs. He grated some cheddar cheese on top and placed the plate in front of me with a newfound energy.

"Wow," I said, taking a big bite of eggs. "I guess this grief group was a great idea."

"I think so, definitely." My dad took his own plate of eggs out of the oven and came to sit beside me. "I needed something like this."

"That's great, Dad."

He sat there and watched me eat like he had something else to say, a secret or a surprise that needed the right moment to come out.

I stopped chewing. "What? Aren't you going to eat yours?"

"Guess who I saw last night?"

"Someone I know?"

"Yes."

"Can you give me a hint?"

"Nope."

"Dad, we know hundreds of people," I said, finishing my eggs and picking up a piece of toast. "I need a hint if I'm going to guess."

"Okay," said my dad, leaning toward me. "It's a wrestler."

"Oh," I said, putting my toast down.

"From when you were a kid."

I pushed my plate back.

"Jenny, guess!"

"I don't want to."

"C'mon!"

I looked down at my plate, at the toast that I no longer wanted. "I don't know," I mumbled. "Jake the Snake?"

"Ha. Nope."

"The Ultimate Warrior."

He stood up and went to the fridge then glanced over his shoulder to watch my face, eyebrows raised like he was telling a joke. "Nope!"

"Dad, I have no idea."

He took a Coke from the fridge and came to sit down again. "Jenny," he said. "It was Joshua Cooper."

My first opponent. His name evoked a kind of tenderness and then, almost immediately, the guilt that accompanied everything else that had to do with wrestling.

I picked up my fork and made little stabs in the toast. "Who died?"

My dad stared at me like the words weren't registering. "Oh, he wasn't at grief group. He was down the hall, another room at the church. For alcoholics."

"Josh is an alcoholic?"

"No! Well, yes. I mean he's recovering."

"Oh."

"But isn't that amazing? Two wrestlers in one building, by pure coincidence. And not just any building. In a church. Isn't this—"

"Dad," I said. "I don't want to talk about this."

"Not even if it's about Josh?"

"No, because if you talk about him, you'll start talking about . . . *it*."

"What?"

"Why do you want me to say it? Why do you always want to talk about it?"

"Because it's what I do all day," he said.

"Then quit. I want you to quit with me."

"It's not so easy to quit. I love wrestling."

I pushed back from the table so fast that my chair fell over, making a loud *smack* on the floor. "Well, it doesn't love you back," I said.

"But it does," he said. "It does love me back. That's what I'm trying to tell you. That's what I realized last night."

I could feel my mouth hanging open. I hated what he was saying. In that moment I wanted wrestling to be an entity, to be there in the kitchen so I could yell and kick and punch it. But there was only my dad. And he was happy for the first time in months.

I ran out of the kitchen into the living room and grabbed the TV, heaving it up off the shelf.

"Jenny," my dad said, following me into the room. "What are you doing?"

"I'm taking it."

I pulled at the TV and the cords caught so that I almost dropped it.

"Taking it where?"

I put it back down and knelt behind, pulling the plug out of the wall, unscrewing the cable. "I'm taking it to my room. It's mine."

I wrapped the cords around my wrist and picked the TV up again, marching past my father to the stairs where I lugged it up, one stair at a time. Out of breath, I heaved it onto my bed and grabbed my backpack.

"Leave it there," I said, coming back down the stairs and pushing past my dad to the front door. "Because it's mine and I want it to be in my room."

"It's not yours," he said. "What do you mean it's yours?"

I slammed the door and took off down the street, but I heard the door open again.

"Jenny," he shouted. "You forgot your lunch."

I didn't even turn around. I didn't want to see his face, though he probably didn't look so happy anymore. I'd taken care of that.

When I got home from school, my dad was already at the gym. I hooked up the television in my room then stayed there the entire night except to get the Ruffles from the kitchen. I left the sandwich and the glass of milk, and took a can of Coke instead. I didn't even answer the phone when my dad called to check on me, something he never brought up, although he did keep calling every night at 6:00 sharp. This is how things went after that. I was always in my room. I never tried his lemon chicken. I left the brown paper bags labeled *Jenny* on the counter.

School was the only thing that was going well because I spent all my time doing homework. My end-of-year report card had to be signed and returned, so I left it on the kitchen table and my dad wrote *Way to go, Kidlet!* beside his signature.

That summer I was usually in my room reading ahead—I'd hassled my teachers for the next year's curriculum—and watching daytime television. *The Price is Right* came on at 11:00 AM and I watched it every day. Bob Barker hadn't aged much since I watched him in the hospital with my mother. This surprised me until I did the math and realized that had only been a few months earlier.

In July, I turned twelve. Uncle Mike came over after work and my dad made a cake out of Betty Crocker mix, but when he cut into it, his shoulders dropped and he stared at it for a full thirty seconds.

"I thought it was the one with the confetti inside," he finally said.

Uncle Mike went to look at it. "Didn't you notice when you were mixing it?"

My dad went to the trash and rooted around until he found the cake box. "It's just white," he said. "I got a plain white one."

Uncle Mike picked up the knife to finish slicing the cake. "How'd you make that mistake?" he said. He cut a huge piece for me and slid it across the table. I wasn't going to eat it, though.

It was getting dark outside. We had the windows open because finally, after a hot day, there was a cool breeze blowing. I could hear the kids playing in the street, staying up late on summer vacation.

"Uncle Mike?" I said. "You know that picture of my mom in the office at the gym? Can you bring it for me?"

Uncle Mike sat down beside me. He'd cut himself a slice bigger than mine and opened a beer. "Why don't you ask your dad?"

My dad was still standing there, staring blankly at the box in his hand.

"Billy?" said Uncle Mike, waving his hand, trying to snap him out of it. "Jenny wants the picture of her and her mom."

"We don't have any pictures of Jenny and her mom," said my dad. It seemed like he wasn't really listening. He was still thinking about the cake, retracing the steps of his mistake. He threw the box back into the trash and got a can of Coke from the fridge.

"Yeah, you do," said Uncle Mike. "The one where she's pregnant."

My dad looked at us like he'd forgotten all about that photo and was alarmed to be reminded of it so suddenly. "Jenny, have you been thinking about it?"

I pushed my fork into my cake again and again, mucking it up, smearing the icing around. I hadn't been thinking about it, not until recently. There was something about the summer that reminded me, and I didn't like the idea of her picture being at the gym without me.

"Jenny, you want it?"

"Of course she wants it," said Uncle Mike.

"Of course she wants it," said my dad. "It's still at the gym. Of course you want it. Of course . . ."

His voice trailed off or I stopped listening. I was trying to remember what we'd done last summer, on my eleventh birthday. But the memory had gone.

That night, my dad knocked on my bedroom door. It was late, around 2:00 AM. My light was off but I couldn't sleep. I ignored him. He pushed the door open slowly and whispered my name.

"I drove to the gym," he said.

I kept my eyes closed, but I could feel him looking at me, trying to decide if I was faking. Through squinted eyes, I watched him come into my room and put the framed photo of my mother down on my desk, arranging it just so. He stood there, trying to look at it in the dark, so still and quiet, barely there.

The memory from last year's birthday came to me: My dad and Uncle Mike and I went out for Dairy Queen after wrestling practice. We ate our sundaes on the restaurant's little patio, and they talked about the opening ceremonies in Moscow because my birthday was the anniversary. Then we all drove home together and Uncle Mike came to our house and gave me my birthday present: tie-dyed sweatbands. The smell of ice cream had come into the car with me and into the house. It stayed on my hands all night. The memory was so close I could've slipped into it.

I thought that my dad was going to leave my room, but at the door he stopped and turned in the frame.

"Sometimes there's a moment where two people split," he said. "And both keep going."

I was so tired, like I was going to sink into the bed, like I was weighed down by a dozen blankets in a good way. I didn't want him to leave and I'd forgotten what that felt like, to draw comfort from his presence instead of guilt. I didn't care what he was saying because I was supposed to be asleep and I didn't have to respond.

"No matter what, we're going to find each other."

I'm not sure how long he stayed and watched me or talked, because I fell asleep.

For years, my dad often came to my room in the middle of the night. He would stand in the door frame and talk. Sometimes I thought he was speaking to me. Others times, I imagined he was speaking to my mother. I never understood exactly what he was saying but I didn't care. It was a reprieve. Because in the mornings, it was like these one-sided conversations hadn't happened. We went back to our strained connection, maintained our distance. But at night in my room we seemed to be different versions of ourselves, versions who were not distressed by each other. I thought about all the other versions out there, the other realities. I imagined that my dad quit wrestling and we lived side by side again, with pizza and television and some new interest like fishing or chess, something completely different that we could dominate together. And there was another one, a timeline that my mind gently wandered into sometimes, one where I won the Canada East Championship and remained undefeated. But that reality was time travel and impossible. I grieved it like a death.

On the morning of my first day of grade nine, I found my dad sleeping in the La-Z-Boy, a book opened across his chest: *The Rule of Metaphor* by Paul Ricoeur.

"Why are you reading that?"

He opened his eyes and looked at me for a moment, waking up. Then he smiled.

"I'd almost forgotten the sound of your voice," he said.

I held my expression without softening and his smile faded, eventually. He said matter-of-factly, "I'm reading it with my grief group. It's been helpful."

I didn't understand what grief had to do with metaphor and I didn't want to acquiesce with more questions. But I thought about it all day. When Uncle Mike called that night, asking for my dad, I knew something was wrong.

"I thought he was at work," I said.

"He's not here. He wasn't here yesterday, either."

"Maybe he's at the grief group. Let me check the calendar."

I went downstairs to the kitchen, bringing the portable phone with me, and shuffled through some papers on the kitchen table until I found my dad's calendar. I blinked, trying to make sense of what I was seeing.

"It says he has grief group today," I said. "But it also says he had grief group yesterday."

"Twice in a row?"

"Uncle Mike," I said slowly. "He wrote grief group in for every day this month."

"He what?"

Uncle Mike's voice sounded far away. I put my finger on every square of the calendar. *Grief Group. Grief Group. Grief Group.* "Something's wrong," I said.

He paused. "I'll come get you."

"Uncle Mike, did he quit his job?"

"I'll be right there."

I locked the front door and stood on the porch waiting for Uncle Mike, trying to stay calm, the minutes moving slowly. I rubbed my arms because I'd forgotten a sweater but couldn't be bothered to go back inside. All I could think about was the calendar. It pointed to something sinister that I couldn't articulate but felt, viscerally: My dad had gone and quit the gym just like I'd wanted him to. But things weren't going to be okay.

Uncle Mike arrived and we drove the ten minutes to the United church in silence. When we got there, the light was on in the lobby but it was very dim. There was a flip chart listing the different groups and where they met. Alcoholics Anonymous was on the third floor. A divorce support group was meeting in the main sanctuary. A youth group was in the west wing. I scanned the list, confused that it didn't include a grief group. And then I saw something else, written down at the bottom.

"Uncle Mike," I said, pointing.

He leaned down to read, squinting in the dim lighting. "Wrestling Group," he said, straightening up. "What the hell is a wrestling group?"

I swallowed. "I don't know but . . . my dad is obviously there."

The group was meeting in the basement so we trekked down there silently and followed the sound of voices to a small carpeted room. There were about twenty people inside, my dad included. They had their eyes closed and were chanting something in unison.

Uncle Mike and I looked at each other. I was unable to speak and he seemed to be in a similar state, swallowing like there was something caught in his throat. We stood in the doorway and listened.

I believe that wrestling is a story, and I believe that story.

I believe that the story is life, and life is wrestling.

I believe in the seven principles, and the one complete principle of one match at a time, one tournament at a time, one season at a time until the championship.

I believe in the worthy opponent.

I will find my opponent.

I will find my definitive match.

I will find the Last Remaining Principle.

I will fight my best fight forever and ever amen.

They opened their eyes. Uncle Mike and I were standing there quietly by the door, not moving a muscle and barely even breathing, but they saw us right away. They looked over at us one at a time until they were all doing it. My dad looked over last. He smiled.

"You're here."

"You don't seem surprised," said Uncle Mike.

"I'm not." He got up and walked toward us. I thought we would duck into the hallway for some privacy but he just stood there talking to us where everyone could hear.

"I figured you would be here sooner or later," he said. "We've been praying you would."

"Praying?" said Uncle Mike. "To who?"

My dad thought about it for a moment. "It's hard to explain."

Most of the people watching us were college-aged. Josh was there. I hadn't seen him in years but he was instantly recognizable. His face had gotten chubby but he still looked like a wrestler, with a boxy stature and permanently stunned look on his face. He saw me watching and smiled warmly. Then I noticed the book in his hand. It was the Paul Ricoeur book from that morning.

"Dad?" I said. "Is it a book club?"

"Just stay for the meeting," said my dad. "That's the only way you can really understand what's happening."

"Is it a book club?" I asked again. I wanted all of this to be about books, even though the flip chart had said it was about wrestling.

"Jenny," my dad said. "I started a religion."

Uncle Mike looked down at the floor. He took a step backwards, massaging his forehead.

"Stay," said my dad, ushering us forward. He added two more chairs to the circle. Uncle Mike went to sit down and I followed, feeling like I had little choice. My body seemed to be moving automatically, numb, a bit like a dream. And everyone was looking at me like they knew me, like I should know *them*, which was adding to the feeling that none of this was real. I had to keep looking at Uncle Mike—his narrowed eyes and suspicious expression—to ground myself.

"We were just about to testify," said my dad. "This is the part of the meeting when we discuss the principles and how they've played out in our lives."

I felt my body curl in on itself, afraid of what I was about to hear. I made brief eye contact with Josh, and then the girl beside him. She was dressed all in black, the only one not really smiling at me, more tilting her head in interest. She met my gaze and didn't look away.

One of the older men in the room raised his hand.

"I wanted to let my church family know that I saw my children last week," he began. There were lots of knowing nods and smiles around the circle.

"It went well. I've been using the principle of Study." He looked at Uncle Mike and me and I drew back, wishing he hadn't. "*Study* means you need to look at old matches to learn how to wrestle better."

He pointed to a TV/VCR pushed up against the wall with a stack of videotapes next to it. I hadn't noticed it until then.

"When you're watching something on film," the man continued, "you don't see yourself, you just see a wrestler. Then you don't have to feel defensive about your mistakes. I've been a disastrous father, but when I stopped being defensive, and when I thought of our interactions, or our *matches,*" he said, putting air quotes around the word, "I was able to act more appropriately, to give my children what they needed."

He sat back in his chair like he was finished and everyone nodded, smiling encouragingly.

"That's wonderful," said my dad. He looked at Uncle Mike and me like he wanted a response. "Isn't that wonderful?"

Uncle Mike opened his mouth and then closed it again without saying anything. He went back to massaging his forehead.

The girl beside Josh raised her hand. "What do you think, Jenny?" she asked. "Do you know about Study?"

I shrunk at the sound of my name. "I guess," I said. "I know about it from wrestling. And I know about the others, too. Strike First. Counter Attack. Endurance . . ." I hadn't listed the principles in ages. I felt unsteady, like the ground was going to come up and smack me in the head. I glanced at the older man, then my dad. "I don't think you should need the principles when you're thinking about how to be a father. I think you should just know how to do it."

"I *knew* how to do it," said the man. "But I couldn't *act* right. Not until I put it into the metaphor." He held up the book.

"Why do you want to make it about wrestling?" I asked. "The

idea—that you shouldn't be defensive—is just true without any kind of metaphor attached to it."

"Of course," said my dad. "It's true with or without the wrestling metaphor, but the wrestling metaphor is true whether or not you know about it or allow it into your life. It's like gravity. If apples kept falling off a tree and hitting you in the head, you would avoid walking under that tree. But if you understood gravity, you would still know not to walk under that tree, but you would know it without getting hit in the head. So, gravity is the principle, and not walking under the tree is the behaviour, just like here, Study is the principle and not being defensive is the behaviour."

"So what's wrestling?" I said.

"In that case, wrestling is science."

"Can't science just be science?" I asked.

"Science *is* science," said my dad. "And wrestling encapsulates science. Wrestling encapsulates everything true."

"But wrestling didn't even always exist," I said. "I mean, it's been around for a long time but if wrestling is *the thing* and everything true is really about wrestling, then how come there's an actual date when it was invented?"

"Truths are truths before we articulate them," said my dad. "They exist in the philosophical realm. Wrestling is an unconscious structure that we're slowly piecing together the meaning of here, in the biological world."

"So, you haven't even pieced it all together yet?" I said. "How do you even know it's wrestling? What if, when it gets bigger, it turns out to be something bigger?"

"It might be something bigger," said the girl. "But for now, it's taken the form of wrestling and we're committed to following that because it's *working*. The principles are true and here, in *this* world. We've given them the structure of wrestling. Wrestling is a subconscious culmination and reflection of everything that is true, intellectually and inherently, known and unknown."

"Well if it includes the unknown," I said, "then how can I argue about it?"

"Why would you try to argue about it," she said, "if it works?"

This was the question. Everyone stared at me, waiting to hear how I would answer. But I didn't know how to explain that I didn't *care* if it worked.

"Let's go," said Uncle Mike. "We can go, Jenny."

"I had depression," the girl blurted out. "Or, I still have it. Maybe I always will. But I'm not fighting it anymore. I realized that my whole life, I wanted to beat it. But *this*," she said, her finger swinging around to point at the room, "made me realize that depression is not my worthy opponent and I don't have to fight it. I went on meds six months ago because of this church."

I looked at my dad, wondering how this had been going on for months and I hadn't realized it. I remembered the calendar and all those squares filled out the same way and how it scared me in ways I didn't understand.

"And I don't feel guilty about that," continued the girl. "Depression was barging into the tournament, using illegal moves on the mat. So of course I was losing."

"And now you're winning?" I said.

"My depression is gone."

"Where did it go?"

"I don't know but it's not on my mat."

"But it's on *somebody's* mat."

"Jenny, we're going," said Uncle Mike. He stood and put his hand out to me.

"My mother died," I said. "She had depression when I was little and she was gone for eleven years. Then she died before I got to talk to her. So what does your religion have to say about that?"

Uncle Mike took my hand and started to pull me up and suddenly we were headed to the door. My dad was following us. We were practically running up the stairs with him behind us.

"Wait," he shouted. "Mike!"

We hurried through the lobby and out the doors, back into the night air, where Uncle Mike took a deep, frantic breath like he'd been holding it. He spun around to face my dad, who'd followed us out.

"What was *that*, Billy? Have you lost your mind?"

"No," said my dad, shaking his head deliberately. "It's good. It works."

I backed away from them, feeling like I would fall down if I didn't sit. I put my hand on a pillar to steady myself, and the door of the church opened very slowly. The girl came outside. She saw me.

"You're really freaking me out, Billy. You need help. And where did these people come from? And you haven't been at work. Do you quit?"

The girl came and stood in front of me, concerned. She was about seventeen with long black hair to match her clothing. Neon socks poked out the top of her Doc Martens.

"I'm sorry that I brought up your mother," she said.

"You didn't," I said. "I brought up my mother." I felt like she was taking credit for something that was mine. I didn't want her to mention my mother at all.

"Well, I'm sorry it came up at all. I just wanted to tell you how much your dad has helped me but I know what happened to your mom and I didn't think about my words before I said them. And now you're upset. And now you're out here instead of inside and your dad really, really wanted you to stay. It's my fault."

"Can you not talk to me," I said, looking away from her and trying to listen to my dad.

"Billy," said Uncle Mike. "Do you quit?"

My dad looked over at me. For a second I thought he could see things clearly. I thought he was going to denounce this church nonsense and come home with us. I thought things were going to go back. There was just something about the way he looked at me, like it was the two of us again. It was a calm moment, like the past.

But then he looked back at Uncle Mike and said, "Yeah, I quit."

"For this?" I said.

"*This* is for us, Jenny."

The calm was over. Uncle Mike grabbed my hand and pulled me toward the car. It was happening so fast. "I don't want to go home," I said.

"You don't have to," said Uncle Mike. He unlocked the car. "Let's go."

My dad was yelling, "How do you strike first at death? It's the Last Remaining Principle. It's the whole point of this. It's what we're trying to figure out!"

I got in and buckled up and Uncle Mike peeled out of the parking lot. His hands were shaking. "Are you okay?" he kept asking. "Are you okay?"

I looked back at my dad. He was standing in the parking lot, watching us go. The girl was standing just behind him.

"Why is she with him?" I said.

"Are you okay?"

"Why is she with him?"

———

I got my things from home—my school books, a few clothes, and my pillow—and moved into Uncle Mike's spare bedroom in the basement.

"Just until your dad gets his head together," he kept saying, but it quickly became obvious that my dad wasn't doing anything of the sort. A few days after we stumbled into his meeting, we started to see a lot more activity at my house. The people from the church started coming and going at all hours. With me gone, it seemed that our home was now a suitable meeting spot. Agonized, Uncle Mike stood at his window, watching and narrating what was happening.

"There's so many of them," he said. "How are they going to fit? There's Josh and that girl who was wearing black." He turned from the window. "You remember her?"

I nodded, trying to ignore it and watch TV instead.

"Religion, my ass," he said. "You can't just start a religion. It's like, a cult."

"Uncle Mike," I said. "Don't watch them. Watch this."

It was *Roseanne*. She could take one's mind off of things. So could *MacGyver* and *Murphy Brown*.

In some ways, life at Uncle Mike's was exactly the same. Like my dad, he worked late at the gym and got home around 8:30. But then he would sit beside me and watch television and ask about my school work. We didn't talk about wrestling. I knew that my dad quitting had been a huge inconvenience for him at work and that he'd had to find a new coach fast. But he didn't mention that. We focused on my future instead. I imagined moving away to university, further from my dad, even as I longed for him to follow me.

Sometimes my dad would knock on Uncle Mike's door in the middle of the night and I would hear them talking.

"I'm doing this for her," my dad would say.

"She's free to talk to you whenever she likes, Billy. I'm not keeping her from you."

"We're getting closer to the Last Remaining Principle. Remember Canada East? I found the tape." Then he yelled into the house, "Jenny, we're studying the tape. We're studying you!"

I would sit on the stairs where my dad couldn't see me. I would close my eyes, trying to hear the sound of his voice without hearing the panicked things he was saying. I could almost conjure our middle-of-the-night, one-sided conversations.

It distressed Uncle Mike. In the mornings, after a night-interruption, he would sit at the kitchen table drinking coffee, massaging his forehead.

"You're thinking about him," I said,

"I'm disappointed," he said, nodding slowly. "I'm disappointed in his . . . fatherhood."

"He's doing it for me."

"He thinks he is."

"He thinks he is," I said as Uncle Mike rubbed his face with both hands. "That's something, at least."

When Uncle Mike wasn't around, I couldn't help but watch out the window too. The lights were always on at my house now. The lawn was full of bicycles and the driveway was full of cars. It was the girl I was most interested in. She got to my house every night around 11:30, always dressed in black. I could tell she was roughly my size, my weight class, even though she was a few years older. I imagined pinning her, as though that would solve something between my father and me, as though the girl and I could be representatives of each side. And I would win. And my dad would quit. And I would never see the girl, or any of them, ever again. And I wondered, how could he tell himself he was doing it for me? Hadn't I been clear about what I wanted?

When he came back to Uncle Mike's house one night, I sat on the stairs and thought about this. I would alter my terms. If my dad would quit this business with the church, then maybe I could deal with him working at the gym again. As long as we didn't talk about wrestling, I could deal with it. I just wanted to go home, sit on my couch and watch TV. I wanted Uncle Mike to come over on Friday nights. I wanted my dad to stand in the doorway and talk to me in the middle of the night while I pretended to be asleep.

"I wanted to give you this," I heard my dad tell Uncle Mike. "I thought you'd like to read it. Jenny too." I heard a thud, something dropped on the hall table.

"What is that?" said Uncle Mike.

"My manifesto. Almost finished."

Uncle Mike didn't say anything but I could imagine him massaging his forehead in frustration.

"Jenny?" my dad called. "I know you're listening."

I considered coming out and telling him my new terms. *I'll come home if you quit the church. I'll come home if we can go back to the way things were.*

"Jenny," he yelled out. "I'm going to Russia."

I froze.

"I'm going with the church. I have to find Ilya."

"Billy," said Uncle Mike. "You can't be serious,"

"I'm serious. This is no country for a wrestling religion. It's different in Russia. It's a lifestyle there. Ilya will understand."

"What about Jenny?" said Uncle Mike.

"That's why I'm here. I want her to *come.*"

"And do what? She's in high school."

"This is more important than high school."

There was quiet and I could imagine them, staring at each other like at the beginning of a match, about to strike. I took one step down the stairs, as slowly and as silently as I could. And then I heard the door slam.

I ran into the hallway saying, "Dad!"

Uncle Mike stood there alone, staring at the stack of papers on the hall table. He picked it up and looked at me. "*The Church of Wrestling*," he said. "By Billy Arsenault."

I darted out the door but slowed immediately once I saw my dad. He'd crossed the road and was nearly back at our house.

"Dad?" My voice echoed strangely down the street. There was nobody else out there and seeing my house behind him—no longer my house, really—was unreal, like looking into the past.

My dad turned. In the darkness, with the dim light from the streetlights, I couldn't really make out his face. He started to come toward me but then stopped when I took a step backward.

"If you quit," I said. Then I closed my eyes, trying to think of the next words.

"I bought you a ticket," said my dad. "We're leaving next Friday. Everyone's going. The whole church."

I opened my eyes and peered at him.

"Dad, if you quit this church thing, I'll come home. I don't even mind if you keep coaching, as long as we don't have to talk about it. I just want things to go back."

"Go back?" he said. "How can we go back?"

I just want to go back a little bit, I thought. Maybe I said it out loud.

There was quiet. My dad didn't say anything but I could read his mind.

First, I have to find Ilya. Then I'll quit.

On the day my dad was supposed to leave for Russia, I stayed home from school. Uncle Mike knew what was on my mind—it was on his mind too—and he didn't ask questions when I said I was sick. We spent the day together, sitting side by side on the couch watching talk shows, hoping my dad would knock on the door and say that he wasn't going after all. The minutes dragged and everything felt grey. We ordered a pizza for dinner, unable to eat much of it, and Uncle Mike called the gym to ask the new head coach to cover for him.

Around midnight, Uncle Mike went upstairs to bed and I started flipping through the channels. He had more channels than I'd ever had at home. I stopped on a show that was immediately recognizable as a game show. It was in a different language. I didn't know what they were saying or what the rules were, but it was familiar. I knew the contestants' enthusiasm and the host's amused but condescending authority. I didn't want it to end, but then another came on right after. I pulled the couch blanket up to my shoulders, suddenly exhausted. It was a game show marathon, I realized, and fell asleep.

When I woke up, the marathon was over and I was thinking about my mother. I was thinking about the photograph of her that I'd left in my room and how it was all alone over there. I went to Uncle Mike's window and looked down the street at my house.

The lights were on.

I went to the front door and darted outside without shoes or socks, running down the street in my bare feet. When I got to my house, I ran up the driveway and burst through the door.

"Dad," I yelled.

But it was the girl in black standing there, stock-still and holding a VCR. She looked at my bare feet and then up at my face.

I pushed past her and went into the living room, which was

empty. The television had been returned to its old place and it was playing *Beavis and Butt-Head.*

"Where is my dad?" I said, turning to face her. She had followed me into the living room and shifted the VCR in her arms.

"You don't know?" she said.

"Of course, I know. He told me where he was going but I expected my house to be empty."

She just stood there holding the VCR. It looked heavy. She shifted it again to her other hip like it was a baby.

"What are you doing with that?" I said.

"It's a double VCR."

"Yeah, I know what it is," I said, even though I'd never seen a double. "What are you doing with it, though?"

She grinned. "I like to tape my TV shows and edit them later in the right order without commercials."

I wondered why I hadn't thought of doing that before. "Well, I like the commercials."

"Really?"

"Why are you even here?"

"I just got back from work. I work at Blockbuster and we're open late."

"I mean why are you in my house when my dad is in Russia?"

"Your dad said I could stay here."

"Why would he say that?"

She cocked her head like she herself didn't quite know the answer. "He's kind of been like a father figure to me?"

"Like a *what?*"

"Well someone's gotta take care of the house, right?"

"What is your name, even?"

She could see that I was getting upset and it seemed to make her nervous. She glanced over her shoulder as though looking for a getaway. "Elizabeth," she said, carefully.

"Elizabeth," I said, articulating rudely. "Did you ever do any real wrestling in that stupid church, *Elizabeth*?"

She shook her head.

"You know you're my size, right?" I said.

She looked down at her body, then looked up at me and nodded, relenting. "I guess so."

"I would destroy you in five seconds." I took a step toward her. I wanted to scare her. I wanted her to drop the stupid VCR and break it.

She cleared her throat. "You probably would."

I was so angry that I thought I would burst into tears and I didn't want to do that in front of her. Instead, I bumped into her on purpose on my way to the door.

"Oops," she said. "Sorry."

I slammed the door and ran back down the street. It wasn't until I got back inside Uncle Mike's that I remembered the photo of my mother. It wasn't alone over there but worse, it was with a stranger. I couldn't go back for it. My father's manifesto was still sitting on the table in the hallway, unmoved since he left it there. I took it into the kitchen and threw it into the trash can with too much force, making a loud clunk. I didn't care if I woke Uncle Mike. I wanted to tell him what was going on in my house, how much I hated Elizabeth, how jealous I was of her VCR.

In the fall after I turned eighteen, I started university in Toronto on a full scholarship. Uncle Mike drove me down and situated me in a basement apartment because I'd opted out of residence, wanting my own space. It was a one-bedroom, with tiny windows up near the ceiling and a backyard just big enough to fit a couple chairs into. He let me bring the bed and dresser from his spare bedroom and we found kitchen furnishings from the Dollarama, and a second-hand couch from the Salvation Army. I had his old television with rabbit ears. I didn't even get basic cable so I was rarely able to watch what I wanted.

My dad had been in Russia so long that his face was fading from memory, but his voice was unchanged and distinct and ever-present in my life. He got my phone number from Uncle Mike and called me all the time. I never answered. Like at home and despite the time difference, he always managed to call around 2:00 AM, waking me up. I let the machine pick up in the living room and listened to his ramblings from my bedroom, his voice coming down the dark hallway like a dream. He talked about the principles. He often talked about the Canada East tournament. I preferred it when he spoke of Ilya. Since I didn't trust everything my dad said, I wasn't sure how close he'd actually gotten to the famous wrestler but I got the feeling they'd had some contact in Russia, encounters that were comforting to imagine. I realized that I'd always regarded Ilya as unreal, like a hero from my childhood, like She-Ra or Atreyu.

Sometimes, after my dad hung up, I would get out of bed and call home. I had been doing this for years, beginning in the weeks after my dad left. I would call my house and Elizabeth would pick up but I wouldn't speak.

Sometimes she would sigh and say, "Asshole," but then stay on the line so I could hear the television in the background, could close my eyes and imagine my living room, my couch. Sometimes she would get to talking about what she was watching, which episode it was and her thoughts on the characters, the story structure. Since I didn't have cable in my new apartment, I liked these phone calls the best.

Uncle Mike had no idea I was doing this.

"She's still there," he said. "I saw her getting in the car on my way here."

He came down to see me almost every weekend. We would get a burger, sometimes see a movie, and have nearly identical conversations to the week before. But this week, he had news.

"I *spoke* to her," he said.

I put down my burger, finished chewing. "You spoke to her," I said, trying to imagine it. They seemed to be from two separate worlds, even though they were right down the street from each other. "What did you say?"

"I said, 'This is my friend's house. The hell are you doing in it, anyway?'"

Uncle Mike took a sip of his beer and for a moment, I thought he was being serious. But then he broke into a grin.

"You should have told her that ages ago," I said.

"Tell me about it. I don't understand why she has to stay there. If it's a matter of looking in on the place then I could do that. Or you could. I asked him, you know. He called me a few months ago and I said, 'Why is the girl there, Billy? There something going on between you two?' And he said no, absolutely not. In case you were wondering."

"I wasn't," I said. "He's more of a father figure to her."

Uncle Mike peered at me. "That's exactly what he said."

"Well, you can't trust anything he's saying, anyway. He's not exactly lucid."

"He says he's found Ilya too."

"Do you believe him?"

"Hm," said Uncle Mike.

"What does that mean? Is that a yes or a no?"

"It means that I don't know," he said, and took a long sip of beer. He got quiet while I finished my fries, fiddling with the bottle, like he was nervous about something.

"I have something for you," he said, after the waitress took my plate. He dug into the pocket of his jacket and pulled out a videotape. He put it down in front of me. The label said *Billy 1975–80*.

Just the sight of it brought back memories, sounds, the feeling of being asleep on the couch but somehow feeling the presence of my dad and Uncle Mike.

"It's a tape with some of your dad's matches," he said.

"I remember."

"Listen," he said, and leaned forward. "I know you don't really like to think about all that stuff. But you should have this. If you don't want to watch it, fine. Put it away somewhere. But I think you should have it."

I picked the tape up, carefully, looked at the writing. "I don't even have a VCR," I said.

"Oh," said Uncle Mike. "I didn't know that."

He looked so disappointed. "It's okay, Uncle Mike. I'll take it. Maybe I can borrow a VCR or something."

"It's up to you. I watched it once or twice. I thought you should have it."

"I'll take it," I said. "I'm glad you brought it."

I tried to smile at him but the image of Uncle Mike watching the tape alone in his house was too much. Despite my best efforts, I turned away.

I put the videotape on a shelf in my bedroom and tried not to think about it. But in the middle of the night, trying to sleep, I could feel it in the room with me. I could vaguely make out its shape in the dark, the white label with Uncle Mike's handwriting. I knew my dad's matches so well that I could conjure them from memory, and in the moments right before sleep, they played in my mind. This small turn toward the past—my dad's past, the time before I was born—was like sleep, comforting and all-encompassing. It kept me in bed. Morning came and I didn't get up. I lost the day.

Around four the next morning, the call came.

Jenny, pick up.

My dad's voice traveled down the hallway and into my room, mixed up with my dreamy memories of his matches. For a moment, I didn't know how old I was. For a moment, I was on Uncle Mike's couch on a Friday night and they were watching the wrestling tapes together, bodies moving with the wrestlers onscreen.

Jenny, I wrestled Ilya! Pick up!

I sat up in bed and looked around my room, time and place slowly coming back into focus. I looked at the videotape on my shelf.

Jenny, I won!

I got out of bed and padded down the hallway, still feeling disoriented. When I got to the living room, I stared at the phone. I could hear the machine running but my dad had stopped speaking. Now background noise filled the room. I heard a car honk, then a click and then, after a moment, a dial tone.

"Dad!" I ran to the phone and picked it up. "Dad!" I yelled into the receiver. He was gone. I dialed *69 and darted to the kitchen counter to grab a pen and a scrap of paper, then dropped to my knees, transcribing the long phone number to Russia.

I dialed. It rang. I imagined him on the street in Moscow, going off to a store around the corner, just out of earshot of the phone. The sound would almost touch him. Or it would touch someone who would touch him. Maybe it would touch some woman walking by and she would go off down the street as well and go into the same store and say good morning to my dad, buying a Coca-Cola at the cash register. And he wouldn't know that the woman was kind of connected to me. He wouldn't really know. But he would kind of know.

I let the phone ring until it cut off automatically, then I sat on the floor beside it and cried. I pressed play on the answering machine and listened to the message again. *Jenny, I won!*

The excitement in his voice was familiar and warm, like when I used to win. I had a rush of longing for those days and then a rush of grief because they were gone. And my dad was gone and I would never get him back.

I picked up the phone and dialed home, my fingers moving without any thought.

"Hello," said Elizabeth, dryly. It was a tone I'd gotten to know over the years, one she likely used only for me and my middle-of-the-night calls.

"Hi," I said.

There was a moment of quiet then she said, "Wow, you can

talk. This must be my special day. What's going on, Jenny?"

"You know it's me?"

"I've known for years."

I was embarrassed to find out that I'd never been anonymous. I was embarrassed and then I was angry that I was embarrassed. "What are you even watching?" I demanded.

"*King of the Hill.* I'm rewatching the whole first season. I taped every episode."

I sighed. "You're lucky."

"Yeah, but this is the last episode."

"So what will you do when it's over?"

She laughed. "I don't know. Try to sleep?"

"Don't you have a job or something to get to in the morning?"

"I work evenings at Blockbuster. I do it for the free rentals."

"That's awesome."

I took the phone over to the fridge and rooted around for a Coke. I couldn't find one.

"Shoot," I said.

"What?"

"Nothing, I'm just out of Coca-Cola."

"Oh. You gonna slip out to buy some?"

"No, I'd have to walk all the way down to Bloor Street."

"Bummer," she said. I could tell she'd turned her attention back to the television.

"Which episode is that?" I asked.

"It's the one where Bobby makes out with Luanne's plastic hair-school head."

"Oh yeah, that's a good one."

"Yeah."

In the pause, I could make out Peggy's voice. I closed my eyes, imagining the show, imagining my couch and living room and Elizabeth in it. Now that I was speaking to her, it felt natural. I realized, regretfully, that she'd become familiar. She was a strange and stable part of my life.

"Listen," I said. "I need something from you."

"From me?"

"Yes, from you. You owe me."

"I do?"

I knew that Elizabeth was indebted to me, though I couldn't put the *why* into words. She was wrapped up in my distress and she knew it. She would do what I asked.

"I need to borrow your VCR," I said. "Can you drop it off tomorrow?"

"You don't have your own VCR?"

"You can drive it down, right? I know you have a car. Or at least you had a car. Do you still—"

"I'll bring it right now. I'll bring my collection too. What do you like? *King of the Hill*? Or *Caroline in the City*?"

"I hate *Caroline in the City*."

"I have tons of shows. What's your favourite?"

"Wait," I said. "Just hold on. What time is it?"

I had a feeling that if she came at 4:00 AM, it meant something for our relationship, which until now had consisted of me harassing her in the middle of the night with prank calls. I wanted her VCR, but I wanted her to drop it off as a daytime favour.

"I'll bring the double," she said. "If you have any blank tapes around, we can copy your favourite episodes."

"The double VCR?" I'd forgotten about it, but now the jealousy came back to me.

"You know," she said. "I have all four seasons of *Friends*."

I caught my breath. I closed my eyes. I saw them, all the friends on the couch by the fountain. It made something cold melt off of me.

"Fine," I said.

Elizabeth got to my house forty-five minutes later. When I opened the door, she was standing there with an overnight bag, a case of Coca-Cola and her double VCR.

"Why do you have a bag?" I asked.

"Because it's five AM and I haven't slept yet."

She went to the couch and sat down, pulling a dozen VHS tapes out of her bag. I went and took a peek inside. There were dozens more, some of them rentals. She had brought me so much television.

"You sure are good at making yourself comfortable," I said.

She looked at me blankly, a rental in her hand. I gestured to the couch, her stuff that was suddenly spread out. "In other people's homes."

She smiled like I had given her a compliment. "What did you want to watch?"

"Let's start with season one."

"No," she said. "You had something you wanted to watch first, right? That's why you wanted my VCR."

I thought about the videotape in my bedroom, the white label.

I thought about watching my dad's wrestling matches and where that would take me. And then I looked at Elizabeth's bag of sit-coms.

"No hurry," I said. "I'll watch my thing later."

Elizabeth began to spend a lot of time at my apartment. She would drive to Brampton for her evening shifts at Blockbuster, then drive back to Toronto with more tapes for us to watch. It was obvious that she was coming over for reasons that had nothing to do with me, but I didn't mind because it was mutual. I wanted to be around someone who wanted to be around my dad. It contextualized the continuous lack that I felt, like an anchor. Having Elizabeth around was an unhealthy comfort, like receding into memory instead of properly mourning. We stayed up all night finishing two more seasons of *Friends* and all of *My So-Called Life*. By Friday, we were halfway through season two of *ER*.

When I went to meet Uncle Mike for dinner, I brought Elizabeth along. We sat down across from him and he stared, recognizing her right away.

"She's been staying with me," I said, then I shrugged because the words were inadequate. How did it make any sense that this person we hated, who represented everything that went wrong with my dad, was now living on my couch?

"But she's been staying at your dad's house, down the street." Uncle Mike spoke only to me, barely looking at her.

"I was," said Elizabeth. "But now I'm here."

Uncle Mike looked at her and sat back, exhaling slowly. "I honestly don't know what to say about any of this. It's not even strange anymore, it's just . . ." He aimlessly waved his hand.

I knew what he meant. *It is what it is.* My dad had left all of us high and dry, and we were scrambling to piece together some semblance of ease. The three of us, sitting together having dinner on a Friday night; it didn't make sense and it wasn't great. But it was the best we could do.

It took Elizabeth and me six weeks to get through four seasons of *ER*. When we were finally done, I had the feeling of a small death.

It was the middle of the night and we went out to my little backyard so that she could smoke. I opened up a can of Coke and took a long first sip.

"I wish we had more episodes," I said. "I like watching it whenever we want to."

"At least it's not over. The series finale is when I really get sad. When *Doogie Howser* ended I thought I'd die."

"What's your favourite series finale?" I asked.

Elizabeth thought for a moment. We were sitting side by side on the steps down to my apartment. The door was ajar, giving us a warm light from the living room.

"Oh," she said, like it had escaped her memory for a moment, but was obvious. "*The Wonder Years*."

"Shut up."

"You don't like it?"

"No, I loved it," I said. "I think it's actually my favourite too. That show was good right up until the very end. And that episode especially."

"It's just so sad," she said.

"Yeah, isn't that funny? How it's your favourite finale because it's so sad?"

"Well, life is sad." She shrugged. "Right? So television should be sad. It's just a reflection of life."

"What about sitcoms, though?"

"The best sitcoms are sometimes sad," she said, "like *Fresh Prince*. Remember when Will and Carlton get arrested?"

"But is it a reflection of life when it's not sad?" I asked. "When it's funny?"

"Life is funny sometimes."

"Sometimes," I said. "But that's not what I mean. I'm talking about the structure of a sitcom and how it all wraps up nicely in the end. That's not a reflection of life."

"Of course it is."

"Huh? How? Life doesn't wrap up nicely."

Elizabeth smiled. "I truly believe that if you *don't* think that life wraps up nicely, you're not paying attention. The sitcom, when it's good, is life distilled into twenty-two minutes. Life is funny, and sad, and structured, and it always wraps up."

"But not nicely."

"Again, I don't think you're paying attention."

"Oh," I said. "Here we go. I recognize this language."

"Jenny, if the sitcom is not a reflection of life, then what *is* it a reflection of?"

"Give me a break," I said. "Now you're just talking about wrestling again."

"We're always talking about wrestling," said Elizabeth. She looked at her cigarette like there was something interesting there. It was simply burning down, untouched.

"Why are you here?" I said.

"What do you mean?"

"Well, if you still believe all that stuff about wrestling then why aren't you in Russia?"

Elizabeth flicked the unsmoked cigarette to the ground, where it kept burning. "I don't even like smoking," she said. "We weren't supposed to do it when I was with your dad."

"I know."

"Then after I left the church, I figured I could do whatever I wanted again."

"You didn't leave. My dad left."

"I left," she said. "Even though I'm the one that *stayed*. I left him in a way. I joined his church. I told your dad that I was going to follow him, that I would do whatever he asked me to do. Then, well, Russia happened."

"But Russia was too much to ask. It was unreasonable."

"Why is it unreasonable?" she asked. "It's not the moon."

"It's unreasonable because everyone is *here*."

"The people that are here were not receptive," she said, a look on her face like she was talking about me and didn't care if I knew it. She was talking about me and she was talking about Uncle Mike. "Religions spread when people move out and go to other countries and spread the word to different cultures, and absorb aspects of those cultures and evolve accordingly."

"Well, if it's so reasonable and makes so much sense then why didn't you go with him? The others went, right?"

"Almost everyone."

"Then why not you?"

It felt like a simple question at first. But Elizabeth sucked in her breath like *here we go* and I realized it was complicated. I could barely answer it myself. Why was I here instead of with my dad?

"The depression came back," she said. "It was gradual, like winter approaching. But then it skipped right over Christmas and settled into that late part where everything is just . . . dirty."

"March," I said.

She nodded. "March. And with the depression comes the anxiety. I stopped leaving my house. Or, your dad's house. The only thing I kept doing was work. I went to work because I wanted more rentals." She looked at me. "So obviously Russia was out of the question. The furthest I could get was Blockbuster."

Then she was just staring at me and I got the sense she was waiting for judgment or absolution and had resigned herself to whatever I doled out.

I shrugged, feeling bewildered, like it didn't matter what I thought about it anyway. "It's okay if you were having a hard time," I said.

"I know it is," she said. "But I told you I had it under control. That time you came to the meeting. I was so confident."

"Yeah, you were pretty sure of yourself. All of you were."

"I miss that feeling. I miss the feeling of everything making sense. But it didn't last. I started . . . floating again, feeling depressed again."

"And that's nothing like a sitcom."

"Your dad is warmth," said Elizabeth.

I closed my eyes so that I could see it. I could see my dad and it was emanating, the warmth that I always felt radiating off of him.

"You felt it too?" I said, squeezing my eyes tight, trying so hard to remember him exactly.

"Yes."

"I thought that was just because he was my dad."

"I don't think so," said Elizabeth. "Everyone must have felt it and that's why they followed him. That's why we were always at your house."

Then I could see it too. Fridays and pizza, television, Uncle Mike and my dad. I didn't want to think about anything else.

But the phone started ringing inside the house. I sat up straight and peeked inside at the clock. "It's my dad," I said. I jumped up and ran inside the house.

There was quiet on the other end of the line, and the crackling sound of a bad connection.

"Hello?" a man said.

"Hello?"

"Is this Jenny Arsenault?"

"Huh?"

There was another pause. "Jenny, it's Josh."

There was more silence, or almost silence. I heard some crying in the background.

"Josh? Are you watching TV?"

"Jenny, your dad died."

I was sitting on the ground all of a sudden. "Huh?"

Then Elizabeth was inside and I put the phone out to her.

"My dad is dead."

She stared at me, taking the phone slowly, putting it to her ear like she didn't really know what a phone was.

"Who is this?" she said, and then I could see on her face that she knew him. "Josh? What happened?"

It was like that time at the church when I worried the ground would come up and smack me in the head. But this time it had happened. I was on the ground and part of my mind had gone slack, fallen away. It was the part of my mind that distinguished reality from fiction.

"Call Mike," Elizabeth was saying into the phone. "Call his friend."

She turned away from me, like that would help, like it would protect me for a moment, long enough for her to get the details.

I understand, I understand. Was he in a lot of pain?

I cried while Elizabeth packed some of my bag. I cried while we locked up my apartment and got into her car, and I cried while we drove up to Brampton, to Uncle Mike's house. It was still the middle of the night, so there was no traffic and we got there quickly. She turned onto my street and passed by my old house and I had to restrain myself from getting out of the car right then and going inside. Part of my mind was so sure that my dad was there, and the other part of my mind was saying *no, he's not. He's dead and you can't go in.* And the parts were warring.

We arrived at Uncle Mike's in a blur and the next few days were indistinguishable from one another. I didn't rest. I didn't want to be at Uncle Mike's house, but couldn't conceive of a place that would feel better.

I thought about my dad's wrestling tape. I hadn't watched it. It was still back in Toronto, up on the shelf in my bedroom. Thinking about it made me burst into fresh tears.

"Do you have another one here?" I asked Uncle Mike. "Did you make a copy?"

"Sorry, honey," he said. "There might be something else, though. If you look through my tapes." He had a bunch of them, labeled and neatly stacked in a cupboard next to his TV. "You might find one of his earlier matches, before 1975."

Elizabeth and I looked. It was a welcome distraction, reading Uncle Mike's handwriting and looking for my dad's name. Some of the tapes were movies that Uncle Mike had taped off the TV: *Lethal Weapon, Kindergarten Cop.*

"Look at this," Elizabeth said. "*The NeverEnding Story*. I should make a copy of this."

I pulled a tape off the stack and before I could read what was on the label, I knew what it was. Like my dad's wrestling tape, the sight of it conjured familiar sounds, and a happy, sleepy feeling. *Ilya—gold medal.*

"Elizabeth, can you go upstairs?" I asked. "I want to be alone for a little while."

"Oh, did you find it?"

"Kind of."

She nodded and went upstairs, taking the movies with her. I put the tape in and pressed play, then went and lay down on the couch, under the blankets. There were lots of matches on there with Ilya winning, some of them almost too grainy to watch. When the Moscow match started, I recognized it right away. I squinted, trying to imagine that Uncle Mike and my dad were in the room with me, whispering about how to win.

When the match was over, I rewound it to watch again and again, pretending it was the old days, listening to the sounds of the sparse Olympic spectators, trying to will myself back into my dad's presence. *Soviet Union is number one! Wrestling is number one!*

Uncle Mike and Elizabeth dealt with the logistics of the funeral, while Josh and some of my dad's followers were accompanying his body from Russia.

"He had brain cancer," Uncle Mike told me, relaying what Josh had said. "He had it before he even went to Russia but nobody knew until he went into the hospital. I don't even know if *he* knew. And they paid his hospital bills."

"Who did?"

"The wrestlers in Russia." It seemed this piece of information had particularly baffled Uncle Mike. "They took him in, Jenny. They all joined the church."

Two days before the funeral, Uncle Mike asked me to go to the house with him to help find some clothes for my dad to be buried in.

"I know you don't have anything to wear either," he said. "You should wear something black."

"But I haven't been there in years and I'm . . ." I trailed off, not wanting to finish. I was scared. I didn't want to see all his stuff.

"I don't want to go alone," he said.

It hurt to hear him make a confession, to ask me for something. I realized he'd never really done that before.

Elizabeth came up beside us. "Is it all right if I come? I have some things there."

Uncle Mike nodded. "Let's just get it done, okay?"

We put our shoes on and trudged over there in a line, Uncle Mike in front and Elizabeth trailing like she was trying to keep out of our way.

In the house, I kept my eyes down. I didn't look into the living room or at the television. I just focused on my feet and went upstairs to my room, hoping to quickly pick out an outfit for the funeral. I knew it would be old and out of date, something I hadn't worn in years.

The first thing I saw when I went into my room was the picture of my mother. I picked it up and tried to wipe the dust off. The glass was permanently cloudy after years of neglect. I flipped it around, removed it from the frame. Then I could see her clearly. *Look how happy she is* my dad had said. And he was right. She looked really happy. She didn't look like she was going to leave.

"Sorry," said Elizabeth.

I turned around. She was standing by the door of my room looking trapped. "I just have to get . . ."

She gestured vaguely—as though she didn't really want me to look—to a pile of clothes, neatly folded on the floor by the foot of my bed. I hadn't noticed it before, but now I looked at the rest of my room. Things were just a little bit different. There was something different about the way the books were arranged. There was something about the way the bed was made.

I put my mother's picture into my pocket.

"Were you sleeping in my room?" I asked.

"No," said Elizabeth. "Or yes. Or . . . maybe." She cleared her throat and looked around. "Should I go?"

She tried to scooch out the door but I stepped in front of it.

"You didn't love my dad," I said. "You used him like you're using me. You believed all the strange things that he had to say and you made it all worse. You made him believe it more."

"I'm sorry," she said. I could see that she would say anything, that she didn't want me to be upset.

Uncle Mike came in with a suit draped over his arm. He held it up. "I think this will do," he said. "It's really old, but I think it'll do."

I looked at the suit that my dad would be buried in, out of style like my own outfit would be. One of us was dead and one of us was alive but we were both stuck in the past, a familial characteristic that transcended dimensions, it seemed. I turned back to Elizabeth.

"For everything you've ever said about wrestling being important, you've never actually wrestled in your whole life, huh?"

She shook her head.

"Well, how are you going to understand the metaphor then?"

I said. "If you don't understand what it's like to wrestle a person then how are you going to wrestle your opponents of the mind or whatever?"

"Uh, Jenny," said Uncle Mike. "What are you doing?"

"You want to wrestle me?" she said.

"Of course I do."

"Here?"

"Yes."

"In your bedroom?"

I took another step toward Elizabeth and assumed the stance, ready to wrestle.

"Wow," she said, almost smiling, trying to copy what I was doing with my body. I reached my hand toward her, trying to intimidate her, and she slapped it away.

"You can't *slap* me," I said.

She shook her head like she meant to focus now, but with her eyes on me she backed up into a pile of CDs, knocking them over. "Wait," she said, like I was already charging. "Wait!"

"What is happening?" said Uncle Mike. "Jenny, stop."

I ignored him. Elizabeth placed her belongings neatly on my bed, then turned to me. I took another step toward her and she circled the room to the other side, doing that thing with her shoulders that athletes do to loosen up. "Wait," she said again, firmly. She shook her shoulders out one more time and took a deep breath. "Okay," she said, assuming the stance.

I charged at her, hugging around her legs and taking her down. She made a sound like the wind was being knocked out of her, and quick as could be, she was on her hands and knees, trying to stand up. I put her in a half nelson and flipped her onto her back and made her bear my weight.

"You have to keep your shoulders up," Uncle Mike said, but he kept his distance. I realized we had no referee but I was thinking we wouldn't need it. I would pin Elizabeth and it would be obvious to all of us.

"Okay!" said Uncle Mike. "Um . . . tweet tweet or whatever, I don't have a whistle."

I got off of Elizabeth and let her stand up. She looked at Uncle Mike.

"Is it over or—"

"Tweet," I yelled, and tried to tackle her again. She sort of jumped back and pushed my head down instead, trying to shimmy away. I got a hold of her legs. Wrapping my arms around her knees, I lifted and pushed with my head until she fell.

"Hey," said Uncle Mike. "That wasn't very fair. I'm supposed to do the tweet sound."

I was pinning Elizabeth and she was laughing. She was all loose and letting me win, or laughing too hard to put up any more of a fight.

"Then tweet," I yelled at Uncle Mike. "I'm pinning her."

"Fine. Tweet."

I took my weight off Elizabeth and she shoved me all the way off. "Get off me," she said, angry but then suddenly laughing again. I stood up sort of victoriously, which seemed to make her laugh more.

"It's not funny," I said. "And you're not very good."

"I know," she laughed.

"You should have moved first."

"I what?"

"I said you should have struck first."

She burst into new laughter.

"It's not funny," I said.

"I know it's not funny. I thought I was crying." She touched her face. There were tears there, and she showed her fingers to me. "See?"

But it still looked like she was laughing. I felt tears going down my own face and touched them as well and showed them to her. "This is crying. This is normal crying. *I'm* crying."

Uncle Mike just stared at us like none of it made sense. And it didn't. It didn't make sense to be wrestling Elizabeth in my room. Maybe in a different reality we would have come across each other. Maybe if my dad hadn't started a religion and gone to Russia and died, I would still be living at home, and would have gotten a job at Blockbuster and become friends with Elizabeth in a normal way. We would have bonded over television, instead of bonding over my dad's exit. I wanted that reality. I wanted that one. I wanted that one. This reality was not worth being in. It made me want to tackle Elizabeth again but she was still sitting on the floor, now full-blown regular crying.

"What are you thinking about?" I asked Uncle Mike, because he was staring deep into the carpet.

He looked at me, snapped out of the thought. "She's not so bad, you know." He gestured at Elizabeth.

"Huh? She didn't even get any points. I demolished her."

"Sure," said Uncle Mike. "But it took you two rounds to pin her. That's more than most of your other opponents could say."

On the morning of the funeral, Uncle Mike drove us, while Elizabeth came along in the back seat. I hadn't spoken to her since the wrestling match in my room. She tried a few times, but I ignored her.

"Okay Jenny," she finally said. "I'll stay until the funeral and then I'll be out of here. You don't ever have to speak to me again."

The service was going to be at the United church where my dad used to have his meetings. The parking lot conjured one of my worst and stupidest memories, but I didn't care. By then it was impossible for me to feel any more desolate.

We went inside and trudged down into the little meeting room. There were flowers everywhere and it was full of people. They were packed in and I recognized many of them. Along with my dad's followers, there were lots of his old students, boys I had learned wrestling with. Around me, mixed in with the English, there was the sound of Russian being spoken quietly.

Pushed up against the wall, the very same TV/VCR from the meeting was still there, like it hadn't been moved in years. I stared at it, losing track of where I was. The videotapes were all gone.

"Jenny," someone said. I turned. It was Josh. He looked different, finally aged, not like an athlete anymore.

I let him hug me.

"Are you angry?" he said.

"Yeah," I nodded. "But not at you."

"Why not?"

I shook my head. All I knew was that Josh still gave me a safe feeling, even though he'd gotten mixed up in the church. "Maybe because you were so nice to me when I was a kid."

"Everyone was nice to you when you were a kid."

"That's true," I said, looking around at so many people from my past. "I wish you hadn't gone, though. None of you."

He peered at me. "I know you didn't buy any of it. But it meant something."

I looked away from him, not wanting to think about that.

There was a man standing behind us in the corner who I definitely knew but couldn't place. He had a mustache like my dad's, like he was stuck in the past as well.

"It's a shame you quit," said Josh.

"Huh?"

"Wrestling. It's a shame you quit. You were really good." He smiled like he was remembering. "I bet you're still good."

I remembered too. I could see it so clearly, hear the sounds. I smiled for the first time in what felt like years. "Well, I beat you."

The man in the corner was looking at me and I was sort of waiting for him to come over and talk to me, give his condolences. But he didn't move.

I gave Josh another hug, sinking into it, then went and found Uncle Mike.

"Who is that man?" I asked, but Uncle Mike just turned and put his arm around me and with his mouth close to my ear said, "You should go up."

"Go where?"

"You should go up and see."

I stared at him. Then I knew what he meant but it was terrible, and I didn't want to.

"Jenny, you should go and see your dad."

We both looked at the coffin. It was right up front and adorned with flowers, in clear view the whole time. The lid was open and I could make out part of my dad's face. It was the most familiar sight of my life, but suddenly the most foreign. It was the very definition of my grief. My dad was here but my dad was gone, and now his face was something I had never seen before.

Uncle Mike thumped me on the back, kind of like he used to, except I was more fragile now, and he gave me a small push to get me going. I could feel that he was following behind, and I could feel that people were noticing and quieting their conversations to watch.

I got closer and closer until I was looking down into the coffin and my dad's face. His mustache had been trimmed all neat and tidy, but it was a little bit grey. This upset me, or at least surprised me, like I had been expecting his face to be the same as when I was a kid, as though a dead body would take the form of its best age. That's what I wanted. I wanted his old face. And it wasn't like I would have ever gotten that again, even if he hadn't died. His old face was gone in any case, but I hadn't mourned it until that moment. The sadness started to overflow, not physically with tears, not physically in any kind of way.

Then I noticed what my dad was wearing: his fifteen-year-old suit, his old and unscuffed dress shoes, and my silver medal from the Canada East Championship.

"Why is he wearing that?" I said, and turned around and faced everyone that was pretending not to look at me. "Who put the medal on him?"

The entire room was looking but nobody was saying anything. There were so many faces that I barely knew or didn't know at all. These were the people with him in his final moments, not me. I clenched my hands into fists and squeezed my eyes shut. These were the people who understood him. I'd given him nothing but grief.

"I put it on him," said a voice, and then all of my anger dissolved because I knew it. I knew the voice from years of watching the same video over and over again, hundreds of times. *Wrestling is number one.*

I looked at the man in the corner with the mustache and I knew who he was. And the realization took me somewhere else for a moment, somewhere peaceful like on a cloud, like on my mother's chest, listening to her heartbeat.

It was Ilya.

He saw me looking at him and pushed off the wall like that was his cue, and came over to me without any ceremony, smiling like he wasn't at a funeral. He had a satchel over his shoulder and a coffee in his hand, filled to the brim. It sloshed around while he walked and I could see that he had spilled some on his white shirt.

"I put the medal on him," he said again, motioning to the coffin and spilling more coffee. "As in, the undertaker carried it out but I oversaw it. As in, I ensured it was done."

Ilya was smiling like he knew something that we didn't, like my dad wasn't really dead but hiding and was going to jump out. They were so similar looking, the same height and build and hair color, the same out-of-fashion mustache. He put out his hand.

"Jenny, my name is—"

"I know who you are," I said, glancing at Uncle Mike because it occurred to me that I might be in a grief-stricken hallucination. Uncle Mike wasn't moving. He seemed to be concentrating on Ilya's face with all his strength, trying to square it with reality as well.

I took Ilya's hand and looked into his face for some sign of my dad, like he would be inside of there looking out, happy to see me. "Why are you here?"

"I brought your father home. As in, I brought his body home."

"You did? Why?"

"Because we're friends. We attended the same church." He winked, then let go of me and began rooting around in his satchel with his free hand.

Uncle Mike came up behind me and put a hand on my back, barely, like he wanted to come into things slowly, like he wanted me to steady him but didn't really know if I was there or not. And I could tell that he was seeing what I saw, my dad in Ilya's face.

"I'm Billy's friend too," Uncle Mike said, putting his hand out.

Ilya grinned, the skin around his eyes wrinkling. Like my dad, he was older than I remembered him. He had aged since the videos that I'd watched, hundreds of times. "Yes, Michael, of course you are." Instead of shaking Uncle Mike's hand, Ilya covered it with his own and stayed like that for a moment, transmitting a message. "Ah!" he said, suddenly remembering and rummaging in the satchel again. His coffee was still sloshing and I took it from him so he could use both hands to rummage. One of them emerged with a thermos, which he placed on the ground. Then he pulled out a pair of glasses. He put them on his head and dug around some more, pulling out a stack of papers and letting that fall to the ground as well.

"What's that?"

"That's nothing," he said, still rummaging. "It's only your father's manifesto, which you've seen before."

"Huh?" I said, because I didn't recognize the words. They were written in another language. "I only speak English,"

Ilya smiled. "It's in Russian. It's been translated."

I stared at it. "Oh."

Finally, Ilya pulled a videotape from his satchel. "And this is the other reason I'm here. Is there a VCR?" He turned to the crowd, which was now watching unabashedly. "Does anybody here have a VCR?"

Elizabeth gave a bit of a jump and the crowd parted for her as she ran to the other corner to fetch the TV/VCR, rolling it over to Ilya and fiddling to turn it on.

Ilya looked at me and Uncle Mike. He was holding the videotape with both hands. "Billy found it," he said. "He found the Last Remaining Principle."

Elizabeth stopped fiddling with the VCR to turn around. "He found it?"

Ilya nodded, tapping a finger on the videotape.

"What is it?" said Elizabeth.

Ilya held up the tape and popped it in the VCR, hitting the rewind button. He looked at me. "He was okay, Jenny, in his last days. As in, he was his old self again."

"How do you know what his old self was?" I asked. "You didn't know the old Billy from before."

"I've known him practically all my life. Since he missed the Moscow Olympics! He was my worthy opponent. As in, he was my . . ." Ilya looked at the ceiling, searching for the right words. "How do you say he was . . . the one I couldn't catch?"

"You mean the one that got away?"

Ilya nodded. He touched his finger to the tip of his nose, tapped it twice. Then he pressed play on the VCR.

The screen was fuzzy, then cleared to a wrestling match, kids in singlets, yells and cheers inside an echoey sports stadium. I was in the center of the mat, eleven years old and shaking my opponent's hand. The match was about to start.

Elizabeth came and stood beside me. "That's you," she said.

"It's the Canada East championship," I said. "It's the day my mom died."

"I know about this day," said Elizabeth. "Your dad talked about it all the time."

"Amazing," said Uncle Mike. "I haven't seen this in years." His hand was on my back. It hadn't moved but now it gave a few thumps, as though he were conflating the two scenes, the one in the present at my dad's funeral, and the one on the television screen at the tournament. We knew how the match ended but he thumped my back like things could still change, like by watching in the right way, my eleven-year-old self could still come out the winner.

I watched the screen with my whole being. I wanted to devour it. I watched like we couldn't watch it again, like I was being granted some reprieve from the way time moved, the way moments ended and then were gone. I wondered if my mother was still alive during this match. I wondered why I hadn't wondered that before.

The referee blew the whistle and we began circling. I could see on my face the thrill of trying a new principle and how nervous I was. My opponent came at me, grabbed me around the shoulders and threw me to the ground. Quickly, I rolled her on top of me and used the momentum until I was on top of her.

"Ohh!" shouted the crowd, both at the tournament and at the funeral. Everyone was watching, they were crowded around, small plates balanced in their hands, speaking English, speaking Russian. Ilya took his coffee from me and put his other hand in his pocket, giving all his attention to the screen.

The referee blew the whistle and we went to regroup in the middle of the mat. Then, for just a second, my dad's profile was visible on the screen. *Strike first, Jenny!*

Uncle Mike laughed. "It's your dad," he said. He looked at me, his mouth open like he hadn't expected it, even though we both should have.

The referee's whistle blew and I was wrestling again. Elizabeth, Uncle Mike and I were tense now, like we had forgotten how it ended. Our bodies moved with the wrestlers onscreen, moved when my opponent threw me, cheered when I countered her, throwing her over my own body and trying to pin her. We held our breath. The referee blew the whistle.

My dad was back on the screen, trying to get my attention, calling out my name until I finally turned and looked at the scoreboard and understood that I was losing. My face changed. My dad's face changed.

I turned away from the TV. I looked at Ilya instead.

"You're going to miss the end," he said.

"I know what happens next."

"Tell me what you remember."

I closed my eyes.

"Well, now the ref is blowing his whistle and I'm frozen. The match isn't going the way I planned it. Nothing is going the way I planned and I don't know what to do about that. Now my opponent has taken me down and I'm still frozen because I didn't strike first and everything fell apart."

"What's happening now?"

"My opponent is about to pin me."

"Your opponent doesn't pin you."

"I know," I said, opening my eyes. "But she comes close."

"Yes," said Ilya. He looked like he was watching something wonderful. I knew that he was thinking about my dad, remembering all the times they watched this match together. I knew about that kind of remembering.

"Look how close your shoulders get to the mat," said Ilya. "Jenny, look at it. You have to look."

I turned to the TV and saw that Ilya was right. From here, it looked like my shoulders were touching the mat. It looked like my opponent was pinning me. But the ref was so close and he could see that my shoulders were up. And my dad was close too. He could see everything.

The time ran out on the clock and the whistle blew. The other girl and I went to the center of the mat. I barely managed to shake her hand because I was so upset.

Then Uncle Mike laughed again. His voice did something I'd never heard before, like he was finally going to cry. "He's looking right at us," he said.

There he was, my dad from 1992, the way I wanted to remember him, looking right into the camera.

The video paused.

"Why did you pause it?" I said. I felt like my dad was about to say something and I was going to miss it. Ilya had his finger on the button, smiling and waiting to speak.

"Jenny," he said. "This is what I wanted to tell you about."

"Huh?"

"Your dad and I watched this a hundred times, well into the night. As in, the early morning. We used the principle of Study."

"Why?" I said, watching my dad who was still unmoving, still looking at Uncle Mike, still looking at us. "I lost the match. I didn't listen to my dad. I didn't strike first and I failed him. Why would you study this match?"

"Because your dad was convinced this was the missing principle. Do you remember the question that the Church of Wrestling couldn't answer?"

"How do you strike first at death," I said.

I wanted him to press *play*. I wanted to be there, in the arena, even if I did everything exactly the same. I wanted my dad.

"Jenny," Ilya said. "You can't."

The picture of my mother was in my pocket. I'd tucked it in that morning and now I closed my hand around it.

"But I want to so badly," I said.

"Me too," said Ilya. "But nobody is undefeated forever."

"But what do I do instead? What did my dad say I'm supposed to do instead?"

"Jenny," Ilya said. He was speaking only to me. Everyone else in the room disappeared. "You already did it. You still are. Your shoulders were so close to the mat. From here, it looks like they're touching. As in, it looks like a pin. But you remember what it was like to be there, right?"

I nodded. I remembered.

"Jenny," he said. *You're good.*

I nodded and nodded. I remembered everything. "I understand," I said.

Ilya pressed play and the past resumed.

Elizabeth," I said. Tears were on my face and blurring my vision. "I felt it more."

"Felt what?"

"The warmth," I said. "My dad's. You said everybody felt it and that's why they wanted to be around him. But I felt it more."

"Of course you did," she said.

I could hear the sounds of the arena, whistles blowing and kids cheering, referees slapping the mat. I closed my eyes because I wanted to stay. It was 1992. I was eleven years old, at a wrestling tournament in Toronto. My mom was about to die, and I had just lost my first match. But I had Uncle Mike. I had Billy Arsenault. He loved me. He was here. He was here. He was here. He didn't say anything but I could read his mind.

That's why you're such a good wrestler, Kidlet.

Acknowledgments

I'm so very grateful to everyone at Split/Lip. Thank you to Kristine Langley Mahler and Caleb Tankersley for the privilege of publishing with this wonderful team. Thank you to David Wojciechowski for the genius cover idea and design. Special thanks to Kate Finegan for understanding this story and guiding it with steadfast encouragement and cheer.

Thank you to everyone who read versions of this story and gave suggestions and/or reassurances: Andrea Kell for always knowing when I needed a serious pep talk; Stephanie Amores for the impressive, television-related fact checking; Iryna Dalyk; Jim Thomas; my neighbourhood writing teammate, Nadia Staikos, who read this story numerous times and encouraged me in a way that nobody else could; and Alyssa Bistonath for her miraculous care and friendship, and steady example of how to go for it since we were teenagers.

Thank you to Dardana Mustafa and Kathryn Decker Malleson, for having decades-long faith in me, and for those early days when we were falling for stories together.

Thank you to my mum and dad for making space for this (sometimes baffling, I think) creative inclination by filling the house with books, reading to me relentlessly, and spelling out every single word of the first book I "wrote" and stapled together.

(And thanks, Dad, for coaching my middle school wrestling team.) Thank you to my brothers, aunts, uncles, cousins and in-laws for always asking, "How's the writing going, Em?" even in the absence of any discernible progress for years at a time.

Thank you, Beanie and Isaiah, for being the strangest, most constant and beautiful source of inspiration and persistence.

Finally, all my love and gratitude to Johnnie. This would not have happened without you. Thank you for the Mani Grant, for learning how to painstakingly critique my work while still, somehow, keeping the peace, and for being joyfully invested in this story and all my stories and our story xo.

About the Author

Emily Thomas Mani is originally from Brampton, Ontario and now lives in Toronto with her family. Her stories have appeared in *The Forge, Barren,* and *Big Fiction Magazine.*

Now Available From

Split/Lip Press

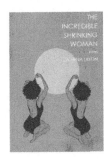

For more info about the press and our titles, visit

www.splitlippress.com

Follow us on Twitter and Instagram: @splitlippress

Made in the USA
Columbia, SC
18 May 2021